THE LAST RIDE THROUGH BHATAN TUNNEL

By

ABHAY SINGHAAL

GullyShelf
COLLECTIVE

First published by GullyShelf Collective 2026

The events described in this book are fictional. Bhatan Tunnel is referenced solely as a geographical setting, and the story does not claim to depict real incidents or documented occurrences associated with the location.

ISBN – 978-81-998235-3-2

Book & Cover Designed By

GullyShelf Collective

For those who drive through the night,
Believing the road will always end.

Prologue

The Omen

The 'food mall' near Khopoli felt completely deserted that night. Usually, there were long queues of cars, families eating ice-cream, and the noise of holidaymakers. But tonight, the weather changed everything.

Harpal Singh finished the last sip of his cutting chai and threw the plastic cup in the dustbin. There was a strange dampness in the air, seeping even under his clothes. Looking up at the sky, his brow furrowed. Dark, dense clouds were rapidly moving from Pune towards Mumbai. A thick streak of lightning tore through the clouds, and a few seconds later, there was a deafening thunderclap that shook the ground.

"The weather's going to get bad, Paaji," said another truck driver standing next to him, checking his truck's tyres. "There'll be a lot of fog in the Ghaat section. Let's stay here tonight."

Harpal looked at his old Tata 1613 truck. It was old, no doubt, but he had complete faith in its engine. "Can't stop, man," Harpal said, pulling a bundle of *'beedis'* from his pocket, but then he remembered he'd promised his daughter he'd smoke less now. He put the bundle back. "It's important to deliver the goods by tomorrow morning. And… the day after tomorrow is Riya's birthday."

At the mention of Riya's name, a slight smile appeared on Harpal's tired face. She was 8 years old. Last month, her school fees were late, so the teacher made her stand outside the class. When Harpal found out, he was furious with himself. He had sworn that this time for her birthday, he would get her the bicycle she had been asking for months. This trip — Mumbai to Pune and back — was going to cover the money for that bicycle.

"Don't take a risk," the other driver warned. "I've heard that these days on the Bhatan road…" he stopped mid-sentence, as if afraid to say more.

Harpal waved his hand, dismissing the conversation. "You too, Shinde. You'll get stuck in these ghost stories. I'm leaving."

He walked towards his truck's cabin. As he opened the door, it let out a long creak, like an old door screaming in pain. The air inside the cabin had that familiar smell of diesel and old clothes. Harpal climbed onto the seat and slammed the door shut. The noise of the wind outside lessened a bit.

He lit an incense stick in front of the small Ganesha idol on the dashboard. Smoke slowly filled the cabin.

"Just get me there safely, Bappa," he whispered.

Before starting the engine, he took out his phone. The network was weak, but the call connected.

"Hello? Sunita?" Harpal said loudly as the first drops of rain had begun to fall outside. The 'chat-pat-chat-pat' drops were hitting the windshield.

"Yes, tell me? You haven't left yet?" Sunita's voice was full of worry. "They're showing on TV here that there's a very strong storm in the ghaats."

"Oh, it's nothing, just a little rain," Harpal lied, so she wouldn't worry. "I'm just leaving now. Listen, Riya's asleep, isn't she?"

"Yes, she just fell asleep. She kept asking repeatedly, 'When will Papa come? Won't he bring the cycle?'"

Harpal's throat tightened. He gripped the steering wheel harder. "Yes. Tell her the cycle will definitely come. Pink coloured. With a basket."

Just then, a strong gust of wind hit the truck. The whole cabin shook. On the windshield, the spray of water was now falling like stones. Harpal turned on the wipers.

Swish-swash.

Swish-swash.

But the water was so heavy that even the wipers seemed useless.

"Alright Sunita, I'm hanging up the phone," Harpal said quickly. "Network is going. I'll reach by morning. Don't worry."

"Drive carefully," Sunita said. "And… that tunnel…"

"The phone is cutting out, Sunita. Bye." Harpal cut her off and threw the phone onto the seat. He knew what she was going to say.

Bhatan Tunnel.

Everyone talked about it. Some said there was a witch there, some said a bride who died in an accident roamed there.

"Nonsense talk," Harpal told himself. He gripped the gear stick and put the truck into first gear. The engine roared to life with a grrr-grrr.

The truck slowly moved out of the parking lot and turned towards the highway. Darkness had deepened. The headlights' glow only reached a few meters ahead, where a wall of rain stood. The road was empty. Absolutely empty. As if the whole world had gone to sleep, and only Harpal was left alone to fight the storm.

He pressed his foot on the accelerator. The speedometer needle started to rise.

40…

50…

60.

Riya's cycle. That's all he had to keep in mind. Everything else – the storm, the darkness, the stories – it was all a lie.

But as soon as the truck started climbing the ghaat, Harpal felt the cabin grow colder. The AC was off, the windows were closed, yet a cold wave ran through his feet. He looked in the rearview mirror.

The blanket kept on the back seat stirred slightly.

"It must be the wind," Harpal thought. "Air must be coming from somewhere."

But there was no wind inside the truck. Just a heavy, oppressive silence that grew despite the engine's noise.

The highway wasn't straight anymore. After Khopoli, the road started climbing upwards, where the black mountains of the Western Ghaats loomed over the path like sleeping giants.

The truck's engine grumbled, straining with effort. The old machinery of the Tata 1613 screamed on every incline, as if begging Harpal to stop. But Harpal couldn't stop. He downshifted from third to second, and kept light pressure on the accelerator.

The storm outside had taken on a different form entirely. The wind was so fierce that even the truck's heavy metal frame was swaying. Raindrops weren't falling straight down anymore; they were hitting the windshield diagonally with a *thak-thak-thak* sound, propelled by the wind, like thousands of small stones being flung. The wipers were working at full power, but visibility was almost zero. The headlights' beam only reached about ten paces ahead, and beyond that was only deep, pitch-black darkness.

On the left side of the road was a deep gorge. In the daytime, this view was beautiful, but at night, in the middle of this storm, the gorge looked like a well of death. One mistake, one slip, and the truck would plummet thousands of feet down.

Harpal rubbed his sweat-soaked palms on the steering wheel. The chill inside the cabin suddenly intensified. This wasn't the chill of an AC; this was the kind of cold that seeped into your bones.

"Gotta reach by morning… by morning," he kept repeating to himself like a mantra.

Sleep and exhaustion weighed heavily on his eyes. To distract himself, he thought about turning on the radio. The old tape recorder was broken, so he listened to FM. He pressed the button.

Khishhh-khishhh…

Only static came from the radio.

Harpal turned the tuning knob. "Come onnn……"

Khishhh… and then suddenly, a song caught hold. It was Mukesh's voice, but it was very faint and suppressed.

"Kahin door jab din dhal jaaye… saanjh ki dulhan badan churaye…"

Harpal breathed a small sigh of relief and turned up the volume. The melody of the song lightened the heavy atmosphere of the cabin a little. He was just about to hum along when the sound suddenly changed.

The music started to stutter. ***Kahin door… door… d-d-door…***

And then, the song stopped. In its place, a strange sound took over. This wasn't static. This was the sound of someone breathing. *Haaaah… Haaaah…*

Harpal's hand froze on the knob. This sound was coming from the radio speakers, but it felt as if someone was breathing right next to his ear.

"Signal's bad," he told himself, but there was a tremor in his voice. He abruptly switched off the radio.

Silence once again filled the cabin. Only the rumble of the engine and the thak-thak of the rain.

But now the silence wasn't the same as before. Now, it had a 'presence'. Harpal felt someone's eyes on his back. It felt as if someone was sitting behind the passenger seat, in that dark corner, staring at him. The same blanket that had moved earlier was now swirling in Harpal's mind.

"You're just tired, Harpal. Just tired," he said loudly, needing to hear his own voice.

Just then, a huge board flashed ahead as the headlights hit it.

BHATAN TUNNEL - 500 Mtrs Ahead

"Alright, the tunnel's here," Harpal thought. "After the tunnel, the ghaats end. Then it's a straight road."

The tunnel's mouth gaped open like the jaws of some black beast. This tunnel, carved through the mountain, felt like the loneliest place in the world right now. As soon as the truck neared the tunnel, the sound of the rain suddenly changed. The sharrr-sharrr of the open sky was now muffled beneath the concrete ceiling.

The moment the truck entered the tunnel's mouth (entrance), the world changed.

The storm outside vanished.

The rain vanished.

The roar of the wind vanished.

All that remained was a deep, echoing silence and the sickly glow of yellow sodium lights casting shadows on the road.

But Harpal noticed the lights were flickering. Every third tube-light was faulty, creating a strange interplay of darkness and light on the road.

And just then, the idol of Ganesha Ji on the dashboard fell with a jolt.

Harpal was startled. The idol was stuck with glue. How could it fall on its own?

He bent down to pick up the idol. His attention shifted from the road for just a second. When he looked up again and saw what was ahead, his heart leapt into his throat.

The tunnel wasn't empty.

A little further ahead… between the light and the darkness… someone was standing.

Harpal's eyes were wide with shock.

It wasn't a hallucination. It wasn't a shadow.

In the dead center of the tunnel, where the hazy light of the yellow sodium lamps fell upon the ground, a woman stood.

She wore a red saree that shone brilliantly, untouched by the tunnel's grimy air. Her long, black hair was scattered across her face, as if someone had flung black ink. She wasn't on the road divider, not on the side, but right in the middle of the lane where a 10-ton truck was hurtling at 60.

"Get out of the way!" Harpal screamed. His voice was trapped within the cabin's glass.

He blasted the truck's massive horn.

PAAAAAN!

The sound was so deafening it could burst a man's eardrums. Bouncing off the tunnel's rounded walls, the horn's echo reverberated even more terrifyingly. But that woman… she didn't even flinch. She neither covered her ears nor looked at the truck. She just stood there, frozen like a stone idol.

The distance between the truck and the woman was rapidly shrinking.

100 meters…

80 meters…

Harpal's foot slammed the brake pedal with all his might.

PSSS-SHHHH!

The air brakes began to shriek. The truck's heavy tires started grinding against the road. The smell of burning rubber permeated the cabin. But a truck wasn't a car that could stop instantly. With such a heavy load, the truck skidded forward, straight towards that woman.

Just then, the tunnel lights began their game.

Flicker…

Flicker…

Flicker.

The lights flickered on and off. Darkness. Light. Darkness. Light.

Harpal felt like he was watching a horrifying film that was stuttering.

When the light came on, the woman was far away.

It turned dark.

When the light returned the next second, the woman had suddenly moved 10 paces closer. She wasn't walking… she was just arriving. Teleporting.

Now she was so close that Harpal could see the creases in her clothes. Her feet seemed to float slightly above the ground.

"O Fuck, she is dead today!" Harpal's mind had confirmed.

The collision was inevitable. The woman was now directly beneath the bonnet. Harpal closed his eyes and, in a final effort, wrenched the steering wheel hard to the right.

"SATNAAAAM SHRI WAHEGURU!"

The truck's balance was lost.

The cabin tilted to one side, and the container behind to the other. It looked as if the truck would overturn any second. The tires' shriek now sounded like an animal's cry. The truck veered towards the tunnel's concrete wall.

Harpal held onto the steering, his bones aching as if they were breaking.

THUD!

The truck's side mirror collided with the wall and shattered. Sparks flew, as if a firework display was happening in the tunnel. The grrr-grrr sound of metal scraping against concrete rattled Harpal's teeth.

But the truck didn't overturn.

It skidded, scraped against the wall, and finally came to a stop.

There was a jolt, and the engine died.

The sparks outside extinguished. The noise of the tires ceased. And once again… that ominous silence returned.

Harpal was glued to his seat, his breath coming in ragged gasps. His entire body was drenched in sweat. He had gripped the steering wheel so tightly that his fingers had gone numb.

"I… I killed her…" Harpal's voice trembled. "I drove her over."

He fearfully opened his eyes.

Beyond the windshield, he could only see the tunnel wall. The truck stood diagonally across the road.

He slowly unbuckled his seat belt.

Click.

Even this faint sound, in that silence, felt like a bomb exploding.

He leaned forward over the dashboard, to look beneath the truck.

He thought he would see blood, flesh, or white clothes.

But there was nothing there.

The road was clear. Only the black marks of the truck's tyres, left by the braking.

Harpal quickly looked in the side mirror (the one that was left) behind him. Maybe she had fallen behind?

The road behind was also empty. The long stretch of tunnel from which he had come was completely deserted.

"She survived?" Harpal let out a long breath. "Or… or she wasn't even there?"

He wiped the sweat from his forehead. "You're going crazy, Harpal. You're sleep deprived. It was an illusion. Just an illusion."

His heart was still pounding, but the fear was slowly subsiding. He thought about getting out of the truck to check, but seeing the darkness outside, he lost his nerve.

"Just get out of here," he told himself. "Start the engine and run."

He turned the key.

Khurr… Khurr…

The engine refused to start.

"Oh man, not now…" Harpal hit the steering wheel in frustration. "Did it have to break down now?"

He turned the key again. Khurr… phusss.

Then… a scent reached him.

It wasn't the smell of diesel. It wasn't the smell of burnt rubber either.

It was the scent of Champa (Magnolia champaca) flowers. Very old, rotten, like dried flowers placed on a grave.

Harpal's hands froze. This scent was coming from inside the truck.

From behind him.

And then, right next to his ear, a sound came. No scream, no noise. Just a cold, wet breath and a whisper:

"What's the Rush??"

Harpal's neck was stiff. He wanted to move, he wanted to open the door and run, but his body wouldn't obey him. Fear had paralyzed him.

The stench of rotting champak (Magnolia champaca) flowers was now so strong that Harpal started to suffocate.

A part of his mind was screaming: "Don't look! Don't look back!"

But that's human nature. When death calls, we always turn to look.

Harpal slowly, inch by inch, turned his neck. His eyes drifted towards the passenger seat.

It was dark there. The cabin light was broken. But the yellow sodium lights from the road, reflecting off the tunnel walls, were seeping into the truck. In that faint light, Harpal saw her.

The passenger seat wasn't empty.

That woman was sitting there.

She was completely still. Her hands were resting in her lap. She didn't look like she had on the road. The red saree that had shimmered from a distance was now, up close, torn, caked with mud, grease, and… blood.

Harpal's scream died in his throat.

The woman slowly raised her head. Her long hair slipped from her face and fell onto her shoulders.

And then Harpal saw her face.

"Oh God…" Only a gasp escaped Harpal's lips.

That face was no longer human. It was burned. The entire flesh on one side had melted and stuck to the bone. Her skin had turned black and red, as if someone had thrown her alive into a fire. Her lips were burned away, revealing her yellow, scattered teeth in a permanent grin.

Her eyes… in place of eyes were just deep, black hollows, filled with a strange resentment.

The woman leaned towards Harpal. Smoke was rising from her burned body.

Harpal tried to pull back, his head hitting the driver's side window. He wanted to get out of the truck, but the door was jammed.

The woman moved closer. Now her burned face was just inches from Harpal's. Harpal could feel her putrid breath.

She opened her burned jaw. The voice didn't come from her throat, but from the depths of her soul—a cold, painful whisper: "You left me too"

Harpal started to cry. Tears streamed down his cheeks. "No… I didn't do anything… let me go…"

The woman raised her hand. Her fingers were burned and twisted. She touched Harpal's cheek.

Her touch was ice-cold, but where she touched, Harpal's skin began to burn.

"Liar…" she whispered.

Suddenly, the truck's engine roared to life with a terrifying ROAR—without the key being turned.

The accelerator pedal pressed itself down, all the way to the floor.

"NO!" Harpal screamed. He tried to press the brake, but the brake pedal had turned as hard as stone. The steering wheel spun, yanking Harpal's hands.

The truck jolted forward and sped away at full speed.

There was no road ahead. Just the round wall of the tunnel.

The last thing Harpal saw was the burnt face of that woman, now laughing hysterically. Her laughter was louder than the roar of the truck's engine.

The truck slammed into the wall.

CRASH!

The sound of crushing metal echoed through the entire tunnel. Shards of glass flew through the air like gunpowder. The dashboard rammed into Harpal's chest.

Harpal's world spun. Pain… so much pain… and then numbness.

For a few seconds, everything went silent.

Harpal's eyes were still open, but now he couldn't see anything. His breath was catching. Blood was trickling down his forehead and into his eyes.

In the darkness, he heard that voice again. Now she wasn't whispering. She was singing. An old wedding song, which now sounded like a death dirge.

"Babul ki duayein leti ja… ja tujhko sukhi sansar mile…"

Harpal Singh took his last breath. His head fell onto the steering wheel.

Silence fell over the tunnel again. Only the hissing sound of smoke coming from the truck's engine remained.

1

The Celebration

There's a different kind of high in a Mumbai night. Especially when you're standing on the 15th-floor balcony of a high-rise building in Bandra, with a glass of whiskey in your hand, and the Sea Link lights twinkling like a diamond necklace in front of you.

Karan Malhotra leaned against the railing and felt the cool breeze on his face. The air today carried the scent of victory.

"Hey, Mr. Senior Project Manager!" a loud voice boomed from behind.

Karan smiled and turned around. Rahul was standing there, a beer bottle in one hand, while with the other, he was gesturing wildly in the air, like some big-shot politician. Rahul—the group's "daredevil." The kind of guy who jumps in without thinking and only later wonders if he pulled the parachute.

"Enough, Rahul," Karan said with a laugh. "How many times will you say it?"

"Until you admit you've become a big shot now!" Rahul came over and clapped Karan hard on the shoulder. "Dude, you got a promotion! Senior Manager at a 'Leading Infrastructure Firm.' That's not a small thing, is it?"

Music drifted from inside the living room. Some soft Arijit Singh song was playing. Priya was sitting on the sofa, typing something on her phone—maybe notes for her next article, or perhaps just uploading an instagram story. Priya was a journalist, always chasing 'truth,' whether it was politics or friends' gossip.
And then there was Meera.
Meera stood in the other corner of the balcony, quietly watching the city. She wore a simple kurti-jeans, a stark contrast to everyone else's party-wear. She had always been different. A little quiet, a little deep. People said she was "spiritual," but Karan thought she just took the world too seriously.
"Congratulations, Karan," Meera said, turning. Her voice was soft, clearly audible despite the music. "You deserve it."
"Thanks, Meera," Karan raised his glass. "Logic and hard work. That's all that matters. Luck and all that is just nonsense."
Meera offered a faint smile, but there was a strange worry in her eyes. "Sometimes things exist beyond logic, Karan."
Karan rolled his eyes. "Here we go again? Don't lecture me today, Meera. Tonight, I want to celebrate."
Rahul jumped in between them. "Exactly! And celebration doesn't mean we stand on the balcony spouting philosophy."
Rahul put his empty bottle aside and looked at everyone intently. His eyes held that sparkle Karan knew well. It was the sparkle of 'danger.'
"What's the plan next?" Rahul asked.
"Plan?" Priya called from inside, putting down her phone. "It's 11 PM, Rahul. Let's order pizza, chat for a bit, and go to sleep. We have office tomorrow."

"Booorinnnng!" Rahul yelled. "Priya, are you a journalist or a librarian? It's Karan's promotion, guys! We can't just spend tonight sitting around at the flat like this."

Karan felt Rahul was right. Adrenaline was still coursing through his veins. He didn't want to sleep. He felt like he could conquer the whole world.

"So what should we do now?" Karan asked, taking a gulp of whiskey. "Go to a club? Lower Parel?"

"No, no," Rahul waved his hand. "The same crowd, the same noise in clubs. Let's do something different. Something memorable."

He leant over the balcony railing and pointed towards the highway below. Cars were speeding by, their red and white lights looking like a long river.

"Long drive," Rahul said. There was an excitement in his voice.

"Drive?" Meera asked, a little nervous. "Now? In this weather?"

"Oh, the weather is the real fun, Meera!" Rahul exclaimed. "Look outside, the rain has stopped, a cool breeze is blowing. Imagine, open road, us four friends, and loud music."

Karan thought about it. The idea wasn't bad. New promotion, new car, and friends for company.

"Where are you thinking of going?" Karan asked.

Rahul replied with a mischievous grin: "Pune."

"Pune?" Priya gasped. "Rahul, that's 3 hours away. We'll be back in the morning."

"So what?" Rahul shrugged. "We'll stop in Lonavala, have tea, go to Tiger Point, and come back after seeing the sunrise. Come on, guys! What's the point of Karan's new SUV if he's only going to drive it in Mumbai traffic?"

Karan put his hand in his pocket and felt the keys to his new SUV. It was a machine beast. He hadn't yet had the chance to unleash it on the highway.

"I'm in," Karan announced his decision. "Let's go as far as Lonavala. It'll be fun."

"Yes!" Rahul punched the air. "Priya? You're coming, right? Or should I go alone with these two?"

Priya laughed and picked up her bag. "I'm coming, just so you guys don't crash the car somewhere. I don't trust your driving at all."

Now all eyes were on Meera.

Meera was still standing by the railing. She didn't look happy. Her fingers were gripping the railing tightly.

"Meera?" Karan asked. "What happened? Are you scared?"

"The highway isn't safe at night, Karan," Meera said softly. "The weather department said there's a storm in the ghaats. And… I'm not getting a good feeling."

Rahul laughed loudly. "Oh, here starts Meera's 'Sixth Sense'. Come on, Meera, ghosts won't come to eat us. We'll go by the Expressway, not some village road."

Karan went up to Meera. He always found Meera's fear childish, but he didn't want to leave her alone.

"Meera, nothing will happen," Karan explained, bringing in that 'Project Manager' confidence into his voice. "I'll drive. We'll be safe. It's just a drive. Come on, please? The group is incomplete without you."

Meera looked into Karan's eyes. She couldn't say no to Karan; both Karan and Meera knew that.

After a few seconds of silence, Meera took a deep breath and forced a smile.

"Okay," she said. "Let's go."

But Karan noticed that her hand trembled a little when she put her glass on the table.

"Let's go then!" Rahul yelled. "Pune, here we come!"

They didn't know Pune was never the destination.

The elevator was descending towards the parking lot. Their reflections, all four, flickered on the metal doors of the lift.

Rahul was still full of energy. He was setting his hair, looking into the mirror on the lift's ceiling. "Bro, the *chai* you get at Tiger Point in Lonavala, it's something else. Plus, look at today's weather! It's going to be so much fun."

Priya was checking her handbag. "Rahul, if it's raining there, we won't even be able to get out of the car," she reasoned. "We'll just drive for 3 hours to get there and then sit in the car and come back. We might as well go to Juhu."

"Negative. Negative thinking," Rahul wagged a finger. "That's your problem, you journalists. Always thinking 'what if'. Come on, live in 'what is'!"

Karan was smiling quietly. The new car keys in his pocket were giving him a strange sense of peace. This car, a gleaming Dark Blue SUV, he'd bought just last week. This wasn't just a vehicle; it was proof that Karan Malhotra had made something of himself in life.

The lift doors opened—Ding.

There was a silence in the basement parking, only the echo of their footsteps. In the glow of the neon tube lights, Karan's SUV stood like a predatory animal.

"Wow," Rahul whistled. "Man, this is a beauty. I'm impressed."

Karan pressed the remote. Chirp-Chirp.

The car's indicators flashed, and the side mirrors unfolded automatically.

"Shotgun!" Rahul yelled and ran towards the passenger seat.

Karan sat in the driver's seat. The fresh scent of new leather still filled the cabin. He ran his hand over the steering wheel. This was a world where Karan was in control. No office politics here, no deadlines. Just the steering, the accelerator, and him.

Priya and Meera settled in the back seat. Meera was still a bit quiet. She buckled her seat belt and gazed out the window.

"All set?" Karan asked, looking in the rear-view mirror.

"Let's roll!" Rahul switched on the music system. Bass-heavy Punjabi tracks began to reverberate in the cabin.

Karan pressed the engine start button. The engine roared to life with a powerful sound.

The car exited the parking lot and hit the streets of Mumbai. It was 11:30 at night, but Mumbai never sleeps. There was still traffic on the roads, but the route towards the highway was relatively clear.

On the Bandra-Worli Sea Link, the car felt like it was flying. The sea ahead looked black, and the bridge's lights danced on the car's windshield.

"Speed up!" Rahul yelled over the music.

Karan gently pressed the accelerator. The speedometer touched 80… 90… 100. The car was gliding smoothly.

"Drive carefully in the ghaats," Meera's voice came from the back.

"Meera, relax," Karan said, turning down the music slightly. "This is a top model. It has traction control, ABS, everything. This car doesn't skid."

As they crossed Navi Mumbai and headed towards the Expressway, the city lights began to fade behind them.

The buildings on both sides of the road were now fewer, replaced by more trees and plants. The light had faded and darkness was starting to set in.

Karan tapped the GPS map on the dashboard.

"What's the ETA showing?" Priya asked.

"Let me check," Karan glanced at the screen.

On the screen, a straight blue line was visible. Arrival: 2:15 AM.

But then, the screen flickered.

For a second, the map spun. The blue line turned gray and a message appeared on the screen: ***RECALCULATING...***

"Signal must be weak," Rahul said. "It happens near the ghaats."

Karan thought, 'yeah, probably'. But then the screen came back.

Now the time had changed.

Arrival: —:—

And the route on the map wasn't straight. The blue line on the map was forming a circle.

Round...

Round...

Round.

As if they weren't going to reach anywhere, just keep going in circles.

"What's this glitch?" Karan asked, surprised. He touched the screen to restart the system.

The screen went black, and then the normal map reappeared. Arrival: 2:17 AM. The route was straight.

"Technology," Karan said, shaking his head with a laugh. "No matter how expensive a car you buy, software is always the cheap kind."

Everyone laughed, except Meera. She had seen that circle.

"Karan," Meera said, leaning forward. "Shouldn't we take the Panvel route? The Old Highway?"

"Old Highway?" Karan dismissed it. "There's a lot of truck traffic there and the road is bad. The Expressway is best. Straight through the tunnel, and then Lonavala."

Tunnel.

The moment he said that word, a slight chill filled the air. The AC was on 22, but suddenly it felt like someone had switched it to 16.

"Feeling cold?" Priya asked, rubbing her arms.

"It's night now, that's why," Karan increased the AC temperature.

But he felt it too. This chill wasn't from the AC. There was something different in the air. As soon as they crossed the toll naka and got onto the main highway, the city noise completely vanished.

Now it was just them, their car's headlights, and the deep dark road ahead.

And somewhere ahead… the Bhatan Tunnel was waiting for them.

2

The Entry

By the time they reached Karjat, the city's dazzling lights were completely behind them. Now, there was only dense darkness along the highway, occasionally pierced by the glow of a dhaba.

"Chai break!" Rahul yelled. "My body's caffeine level is dropping."

Karan stopped the car in front of a big, brightly lit dhaba—'Sher-e-Punjab Dhaba'. Several trucks were parked outside, their colorful designs and slogans written on their horns gleaming in the tube-light. The air carried a mixed scent of tandoori roti, daal makhani, and diesel.

All four of them got out of the car. Karan stretched, cracking the bones in his back. The cold outside had intensified. Priya wrapped her stole tightly around herself.

"Wait two minutes, I'll place the order," Karan said and headed towards the counter.

The other three went and sat down on the charpais kept outside. Nearby, a group of truck drivers was sitting. Their faces were tired, their clothes dirty, and they held hot chai glasses in their hands. They were talking amongst themselves in low voices, but the atmosphere felt serious.

Meera's attention was drawn to them. They weren't laughing. They looked scared.

"...I'm not lying, bro," a driver with a white beard was saying. "It happened with Harpal just last night. police is saying the brake failed, but I saw the truck's condition. It looked as if someone had... melted the truck from the inside."

Rahul nudged Meera with his elbow and chuckled softly. "Listening? Their horror stories are starting."

But Meera gestured to Rahul to be quiet. She wanted to listen.

Another driver, who was a bit younger, looked around nervously. "People say she's in Bhatan Tunnel. She asks for a lift. She stands there in a red saree."

"Lift?" Priya interrupted. Her journalist's instinct had awakened. She got up and walked towards the drivers. "Excuse me, who are you talking about?"

The group of drivers fell silent. They looked at these city 'rich kids' from head to toe.

The old driver glared. "Madam ji, this is none of your business. You people go, have your party."

"No, tell us," Rahul also came behind, in a teasing tone. "Who asks for a lift? Is she a beautiful girl? If she's beautiful, I'd definitely stop the car."

Karan returned with the chai glasses and, hearing Rahul's comment, laughed. "Rahul, enough. Why are you bothering the poor people? These are just stories so these guys stay awake all night. Fear is the best way to drive away sleep."

The old driver stood up. There was no anger in his eyes, but a strange sadness.

"Don't joke around, Sir," he said in a heavy voice. "That's not just a story. That's Shalini."

"Shalini?" Meera whispered.

"She was a bride," the driver explained, his voice trembling. "Years ago, on this very highway, on her wedding night. Her groom left her on the roadside after an argument. She was alone, asking for help."

"A speeding car came… ran her over and left. No one stopped. Everyone left her there to die."

The driver took a step forward and looked straight into Karan's eyes.

"Since then, she's been here. She asks for a lift. If you stop the car, she gets in and takes your life. If you don't stop… she forces her way in."

Karan placed his tea glass on the table. He thought this man was crazy. "Okay, old man. Good story. But we need to go. Come on, guys."

Karan turned and started walking towards his car. Priya and Rahul, suppressing their laughter, followed him.

But Meera stayed there. She felt like the driver was telling the truth. The air had suddenly become heavy.

The old driver grabbed Meera's hand. Meera got scared.

"Daughter," he said softly. "Don't go. Wait for morning. She's angry tonight. She took Harpal… now she's looking for someone else."

"Leave her!" Karan yelled, coming back and swatting the driver's hand away. "Don't touch her. Are you people crazy? Meera, get in the car. Now."

Meera's breathing had quickened. "Karan, they're warning us…"

"Meera, please!" Karan was angry. "We haven't come here to listen to some illiterate driver's ghost story. Get in the car."

Karan forcefully pushed Meera towards the car.

As soon as they got into the car and closed the door, the noise outside stopped. Karan started the engine and angrily pressed the accelerator. The SUV roared out of the dhaba, kicking up dust, and was back on the dark highway.

Behind them, the old driver was still standing there. He clasped his hands together and closed his eyes, as if he was praying for them.

Inside the car, the atmosphere was a bit tense.

"Ugh, this ruined my mood," Rahul complained. "These people scare you for no reason."

"But his eyes…" Priya said softly, no longer taking notes. "He really looked scared."

"Mass hysteria," Karan rationalized. "One person lies, everyone else believes it. It's psychology, Priya. You know that."

Meera was quietly looking out the window. She could see her face in the glass, but it felt like someone else was also racing with her in the darkness.

Just then, the digital clock on the dashboard started blinking.

11:59 PM.

12:00 AM.

As soon as it struck midnight, the radio turned on by itself.

Kharrrr-kharrrr… (Static noise).

"Hey, I didn't turn this on," Karan said in surprise. He pressed the off button. The radio didn't turn off.

Through the static, a sound emerged. It wasn't a song, just the sound of a woman crying. Faint, painful sobs.

Meera's heart pounded. "Karan, stop the car."

"Signal issue, Meera," Karan tried to lower the volume, but the volume knob wasn't working.

"Karan, please!" Meera screamed.

Suddenly, a board appeared on the road ahead, shining in the headlights:

BHATAN TUNNEL: 1 KM.

"There," Rahul said, "Here comes your haunted tunnel. Let's see which bride asks for a lift."

But this time, even Rahul's voice lacked that former confidence.

The temperature inside the car suddenly dropped. Their breaths now appeared like fog.

Karan gripped the steering wheel tightly. "It's all nonsense," he told himself. "Just a tunnel."

But he was wrong. It wasn't a tunnel. It was a mouth, open to swallow them whole.

The mouth of the Tunnel was now directly in front of them. The concrete structure, carved into the mountain, looked like the throat of some giant beast, ready to swallow them whole. The yellow sodium lights inside the tunnel were a stark contrast to the deep darkness outside. It wasn't the usual street light glow; it was a sickly, dim, flickering light.

"Hold on tight," Karan said, forcing confidence into his voice. "We're just crossing."

The moment the SUV entered the tunnel, the world changed.

WHOOSH.

The roar of the outside air vanished, replaced by the distinct echoing hum of the tunnel. The sound of the tires now came back as a hummm-hummm, bouncing off the walls. Inside the car, the radio's static had grown so loud it made their ears ache.

Kharrrr… CHIKHH… Kharrrr…

"Turn it off, Karan!" Priya cried, covering her ears. "I can't stand this noise!"

Karan, in a fit of anger, punched the power button to shut off the entire infotainment system. The screen went black. The noise stopped.

For a second, silence filled the car.

"Thank God," Rahul breathed a sigh of relief. "Damn radio."

But that relief was fleeting.

Meera, who had been silent until now, suddenly shrieked: "WHAT IS THAT?!"

She pointed a finger towards the front windshield.

Karan looked ahead. In the middle of the tunnel, the lights were flickering. Sometimes dark, sometimes bright. And in the midst of this play of light… there was something.

At first, it was just a red blur. Then, as the car got closer, it became clear.

A woman.

She wasn't hanging upside down from the tunnel's ceiling, nor was she floating in the air. She stood in the middle of the road, absolutely still. Her back was towards the car. Her long black hair reached her waist.

"Get out of the way!" Karan instinctively honked and switched the headlights to high-beam.

The light fell upon the woman.

The woman turned around.

It was the same face that the truck driver Harpal had seen. Burnt flesh. Melted skin. And those large, black eyes that held an ocean of death.

"Mummy!" Rahul screamed.

Karan's mind went numb. He wanted to hit the brakes, but the car was moving at 100 km/hr. He jerked the steering wheel to the left.

"NOOO!" Meera's scream echoed through the car.

The SUV's tires skidded on the road.

SCREEEEEECH!

The car lost control. It spun around. The world started spinning rapidly—Tunnel lights, wall, darkness, lights, wall…

The concrete wall ahead was rushing towards them.

Just before impact, Karan saw the woman standing there, smiling. And inside the car, a voice shrieked from the dead radio:

"YOU'VE ARRIVED…"

DHADAAAAM!

There was a mighty explosion.

Metal crumpled. Glass shattered in the air. There was a POOF as airbags deployed. Karan's head slammed into the steering wheel. Priya and Meera fell on top of each other. Rahul's head hit the dashboard.

The car flipped.

Once.

Twice.

Sparks flew up to the tunnel ceiling. The car skidded, flipped over, and finally stopped.

One wheel was still spinning in the air… Whirrr… whirrr…
Then… silence.
A deep, absolute silence.
No screams. No crying. No pain.
Just that yellow light from the tunnel, now seeping in through the shattered windows of the overturned car. Smoke and dust hung in the air.
Darkness fell.
(Fade to Black)

3

The Awakening

Tiiiiinnnnnnnnn…

That sound wasn't coming from outside. It was ringing inside Karan's brain. Like a broken radio signal—a long, sharp, ear-splitting whistle.

Karan opened his eyes, but he couldn't see anything. He thought maybe he had gone blind, or perhaps the tunnel lights had gone out. He tried to breathe. The air was heavy. It carried the sharp stench of burnt rubber, hot metal, and gunpowder—the smell that comes when airbags deploy. This stench caught in his throat, making him cough.

Khukh… Khukh…

The sound of his cough broke the silence.

Karan moved his hands. His fingers could feel the leather of the steering wheel. He was there. In the driver's seat.

"I… I… am I alive?" he whispered. His own voice sounded like a stranger's to him—heavy and distant.

Memory came back like shattered glass.

That woman…

in the middle of the road…

burnt face…

swerving the steering wheel…

the screech of tires…

the world spinning…

And the explosion.

The explosion was so powerful that he should have died. The car had flipped—he distinctly remembered the car flipping. The roof was down and the ground was up. But how?

Karan frantically fumbled around him. The car was upright. The roof was above. The seatbelt still held him tight.

"A dream?" Karan thought. "Did I have a dream after hitting my head?"

He touched his face with his hand. Forehead, nose, cheeks. Everything was intact. No deep wounds, no bleeding. Yes, his skin was a bit cold, ice cold, but the pain was gone.

That's when his friends came to mind.

"Rahul? Priya?" Karan tried to turn back. A crack came from his neck, but there was no pain.

In the darkness, with the help of the tunnel's flickering sodium lights, he saw everyone else.

Rahul was slumped sideways in the passenger seat. His head was resting on the dashboard's glove box. He wasn't moving.

"Rahul!" Karan screamed. He grabbed Rahul's shoulder and shook him violently. "Rahul, wake up, buddy! Please, wake up!"

There was no movement in Rahul's body. Karan's heart pounded—or at least he thought it was pounding. Had he killed his best friend? Was this drive their last mistake?

Karan placed his finger near Rahul's nose. Was he breathing? He couldn't tell. His own fingers were so numb that he couldn't feel anything.

"Meera! Meera, are you okay?" Karan looked back.

Meera was slumped behind the front seat. Her eyes were open. She was staring straight ahead without blinking, gazing at some invisible thing in the darkness of the tunnel.

"Meera?" Karan called out a little louder.

Meera slowly, robotically, turned her head. There was no fear in her eyes, but rather a strange emptiness.

"We stopped," Meera said slowly. Her voice was completely flat.

"Yes, we stopped."

"An accident happened," Karan said quickly, feeling a little relieved that at least Meera was speaking.

Just then, Rahul took a long, gasping breath—HAAA-UH!—like someone emerging from underwater.

Rahul shot upright with a jolt, flailing his arms and legs in the air. "Help! She's coming! She's coming!"

"Shhh! Rahul, calm down!" Karan grabbed his arm. "We're okay. Look, the car has stopped. We're safe."

Rahul stared at Karan with wide eyes, then looked around. He ran a hand over his chest, then his head. "My head… it hit the dashboard…" he said, bewildered. "It hit really hard."

"Is it bleeding?" Karan asked, fumbling for his mobile flashlight.

Rahul rubbed his forehead. "No. It doesn't even hurt. It's weird… I thought my skull would have cracked open."

"Adrenaline," Karan offered the same old logic, though he himself couldn't quite believe it. "You're not feeling the pain because of the shock. You'll feel it later."

From the back, Priya's stirring sound was heard. She was sitting up in her seat, adjusting her hair.

"Guys?" Priya's voice was trembling. "Were… were we about to die?"

"We're safe, Priya," Karan emphasized. "Just a spin. Maybe the car skidded."

Karan unbuckled his seatbelt.

Click.

The sound felt like a bomb blast in that silence.

He tried to pull the handle to open the door. The door was jammed. The metal had probably bent. He pushed it with his shoulder.

Thud.

The door rattled, but didn't open.

"The doors are probably locked because of the crash," Karan said, hiding his panic. "I'll roll down the window."

He pressed the power window button.

Nothing happened.

The car's entire electrical system was dead. The dashboard was dark. The AC was off. The music system was off.

"Battery's gone," Karan slammed his hand on the steering wheel. "Damn it! It was a new car."

Now that the noise had stopped and they were conscious, they realized how quiet the tunnel was.

This wasn't the kind of quiet that falls at night. This was a 'death-like' quiet.

On the expressway, there's always the vroom-vroom sound of vehicles. The wind blows. There are sounds of insects.

But here? Nothing.

As if someone had pressed the 'Mute' button on the world.

Dust particles floated in the tunnel air, shimmering in the yellow lights.

"Where's the traffic?" Rahul asked, looking out the window. "We've been here for 5 minutes. Some truck, some bus should have come by now?"

Karan also noticed. Both ends of the tunnel were dark. Looking back, the tunnel's mouth (entrance) should have been visible, but there was only something like black smoke.

"The road must be blocked," Karan rationalized. "Maybe traffic behind us was stopped because of our crash."

"Or maybe…" Meera whispered, "…we are in a place where no one else can come."

"Meera, please," Karan snapped. "Don't start all that now. We need to get out."

Karan pressed the ignition button again.

Click.

Click.

The engine gave no response.

The cold inside the cabin was increasing. Fog started to accumulate on the windows.

Priya leaned forward, between the two seats. "I… I feel something wet."

"The water bottle must have fallen," Rahul said.

"No," Priya touched her nose and looked at her fingers. The color wasn't clearly visible in the dark, but it was like a thick paste.

"This… this is blood," Priya's voice was like a child's, utterly terrified and weak.

She held her hand towards the light—or whatever illumination was coming from the tunnel's flickering lights. Her fingers were stained dark crimson.

"Oh shit," Rahul leaned forward from the backseat. "Priya, your nose… it's not stopping."

Priya fumbled in her bag, pulling out a whole bundle of tissues and pressing them to her nose. The tissue turned red in an instant. The blood wasn't just flowing, it was dripping, tap-tap-tapping, onto her expensive jeans.

"Does it hurt?" Karan asked, his mind still searching for logic. "Is it fractured somewhere?"

Priya shook her head, her eyes filled with tears. "I don't feel anything, Karan. It's completely numb. It's just… bleeding."

Meera, who had been as still as a statue until now, suddenly spoke. "The body doesn't hurt after it breaks, Priya. It hurts when…"

"Shut up, Meera!" Karan yelled. His patience was wearing thin. "Right now we need first-aid, not philosophy."

Karan put all his weight on his door. "Open up, damn it!"

He pushed with his shoulder.

CRACK.

The door lock broke, or maybe the metal melted—that's what the sound was like. The door opened with a strange squeal, and Karan stumbled out, falling onto the road.

He quickly stood up.

The air outside… was wrong.

The air on an expressway always has a mixture of dust, petrol, and coolness. But this tunnel air was stale. As if a closed room had been opened after years. It was humid, and had that faint, rotting scent of champa flowers that had just begun.

“Everyone get out,” Karan bent inside and said. “It’s not safe to stay here.”

Rahul and Priya also pushed and shoved their way out. Meera was the last to emerge. She stood pressed against the tunnel wall, as if she was afraid to touch the road.

Karan went to the front of the car. To check the bonnet.

“I’ll check the engine,” he said. “Maybe the battery got loose.”

He placed his hand on the bonnet.

And he recoiled in shock.

“It’s cold…” Karan whispered.

“What?” Rahul came closer.

“The bonnet,” Karan said in surprise. “We were driving at 100 speed. The engine should be hot. My hand should be burning. But this… this is cold as ice. Like the car has been parked for hours.”

“Karan, what’s happening?” Priya started crying, still pressing the tissue to her nose. “Where’s the traffic? Where are the people? Why there is no network in the phone?”

Karan had no answer. He looked around nervously. His gaze fell on the driver side’s Side-View Mirror.

The mirror was a little crooked because of the crash. Karan’s face was visible in it.

Karan looked in the mirror to fix his hair. There was a little dust on his forehead, and fear in his eyes.

He was about to turn away when… something happened in the mirror.

Karan’s reflection didn’t move.

The real Karan had turned away, but the mirror Karan was still staring straight ahead.

Karan's blood ran cold. He slowly turned back towards the mirror.

The Karan inside the mirror was glaring at him. The reflection's eyes were wider than Karan's. And slowly… a smile appeared on the reflection's lips.

A very nasty, devilish smile.

The real Karan opened his mouth to scream, but no sound came out.

The mirror Karan opened his mouth. And without making a sound, he moved his lips:

"Liar…"

And then, the reflection started laughing. No sound came out, but his laughter was so terrifying that Karan felt like his brain would

explode. The reflection was banging his head on the dashboard and laughing, while the real Karan stood outside, trembling.

"Karan? What happened?" Rahul grabbed his shoulder.

Karan recoiled with a jolt, as if he'd been electrocuted. "That… in the mirror…"

He pointed a finger.

Rahul looked in the mirror. "What is it? It's just broken."

Karan gathered courage and looked back.

The reflection was normal. The same dusty face, the same scared Karan standing next to Rahul.

"Nothing," Karan took a long breath, though his heart was still in his throat. "Just… my mind is messed up."

He moved away from the car and stood in the middle of the road.

Now all four of them realized how alone they were.

The tunnel was dark ahead, and dark behind. Where they had come from, there should have been light, but now there was only a hazy black wall.

The radio, which had been off inside the car, suddenly started crackling again. With the doors open, the sound was clearly audible outside.

Kharrrr…

This time it wasn't static. This time it was a man's voice. A news reporter's voice.

"…a terrible accident occurred this morning in Bhatan Tunnel. Four people died on the spot. Police said that the car was so badly burned that it was difficult to identify the bodies…"

The radio's voice continued to echo.

Priya dropped the tissue. "This… this news… is this about us?"

"Shut up with the nonsense!" Karan yelled, ran towards the car, and punched the radio panel. "Shut up! Shut up!"

But the sound didn't stop. It got even louder.

"…the names of those killed are: Karan Malhotra, Rahul Verma, Priya Sharma…"

"NO!" Karan smashed the infotainment screen with all his might. Glass shards scattered, and finally the sound stopped.

Silence returned.

But this calm was more dangerous than before. Because now they knew. This 'Isolation' was not normal.

The world had moved on without them.

Meera sat down on the road, hugging her knees. "We are alone," she said softly, her voice echoing in the tunnel. "No one is coming, Karan. No one is coming."

Karan looked around. Only concrete, darkness, and that flickering sickly light.

They were cut off from the world. And now, in this darkness, they were not alone.

From the depths of the tunnel… the sound of anklets began to jingle.

Chann… Chann…

Chann…

4

Purgatory

Chann… Chann… Chann…

That sound wasn't like music. It was heavy, burdensome. Like iron chains dragging across concrete. In the deep silence of the tunnel, every 'Chann' hit their ears like a hammer.

"Who's there?" Karan yelled. The earlier strength was gone from his voice. He was just a terrified animal, yelling to save himself.

No answer came from the darkness. Only that sound drew closer.

Meera, who had been sitting on the road until now, slowly stood up. She looked towards the part of the tunnel where the darkness was deepest.

"She's here," Meera whispered. "The bride is here."

"Shut up, Meera!" Rahul said angrily. He was scared, and his fear was turning into anger. He picked up an iron rod (jack handle) from near the car's broken door. "Whoever you are, come out! I have a weapon!"

Just then, the tunnel lights flickered again.

Zzzzt…

When the light came back on, she was there.

About 50 paces away from them.

She stood in the middle of the road.

Red saree.

Long black hair covering her face.

But this time something was different. Her clothes were billowing in the air, even though there was no wind in the tunnel.

"Hey!" Rahul waved the rod in the air. "Stay away! We're calling the police!"

The woman didn't move. She just tilted her head a little, like a predator observing its prey.

And then, she started to move.

Her steps didn't seem to touch the ground; she just moved forward.

Chann… Chann…

As she came closer, that stench returned. Rotten Champa and burnt flesh. This smell was so strong that Priya tried to vomit, but her stomach was empty.

"Rahul, step back," Karan tried to pull Rahul. "This… this is not human."

"I'm not afraid of her!" Rahul yelled, trying to hide his fear. He moved forward. "I said, stay away!"

Rahul threw the iron rod with all his might towards the woman.

The rod flew spinning through the air, straight towards her head. The aim was perfect.

But just before impact, the rod stopped in mid-air.

As if an invisible hand had caught it.

That heavy iron rod hung there in the air, defying the laws of gravity.

Rahul's eyes were wide with disbelief. "How… how is this possible…"

The woman slowly raised her hand. The rod spun in the air, and flew back rapidly towards Rahul.

SWISH!

Rahul ducked. The rod passed over his head and hit the remaining glass of the car behind them—

SHATTER!

“Run!” Karan yelled. “Hide behind the car!”

All four stumbled and ran towards their overturned car. They hid behind the car’s body, trembling violently.

“What is this thing?” Priya was crying, her blood now reaching her lips. “Where have we gotten ourselves into?”

“We’re dead,” Meera finally spoke the most terrifying truth. “The radio said… we’re dead. This is hell.”

“No!”

Karan grabbed Meera and shook her. “We’re alive! The radio was broken! That news was fake! We’re right here, breathing!”

Just then, right above them, they heard someone walking on the car’s roof.

Thump… Thump…

That woman was now on top of the car.

Priya shrieked and clapped her hand over her mouth.

A burnt, black hand reached in through the car’s broken window and grabbed Priya’s hair.

“AAAAAHHH!” Priya screamed.

That hand was pulling her upwards. Priya’s feet began to lift off the ground.

“Hold her!” Rahul and Karan grabbed Priya’s legs. They were playing tug-of-war—on one side, two men, and on the other, that unknown force.

“Leave me!” Priya shrieked.

From above came the same voice, which was no longer a whisper, but a growl:

"Fake news…

Fake story…

Where is the truth, Priya?"

Priya's face went white.

That force wasn't just to kill her; it was to remind her.

"Rahul, Karan, Save me!" Priya started crying. " Leave me!"

As soon as Priya shouted, the grip loosened.

The woman's hand disappeared.

Priya fell to the ground, panting heavily. The burnt handprints were etched onto her neck—black and red.

Silence returned.

But now that woman wasn't on top of the car.

She was standing in front of them now. Right in front.

The car's headlights (which had broken in the crash but now suddenly switched on) shone on her face.

For the first time, they saw her face clearly.

It was burnt, yes.

But beneath that burnt flesh, features were visible. She must have been beautiful once. Her eyes were glaring at them.

Karan, who until now had been the most skeptical, now fell to his knees. His logic, his science, everything had failed.

The woman pointed a finger at Karan.

"You…" her voice echoed, bouncing off the tunnel walls. "You didn't believe, did you?"

No sound came from Karan's mouth.

"Now you will believe," the woman said. "When your turn comes."

Suddenly, the woman let out a loud, piercing scream. That scream was not human. It was pure 'frequency'.

SCREEEEEEECH!

All the tunnel lights burst simultaneously.

POP-POP-POP-POP!

It rained glass.

And then… pitch darkness.

This time the darkness was different. This time she wasn't alone in the darkness. Now there were thousands of whispers in the darkness.

"We have to get inside the car," Rahul whispered. "Outside, we're open targets."

"The car is locked!" Karan reminded him.

"Get in through the broken window!" Rahul commanded. "Quick!"

In the darkness, fumbling, all four began to scramble back inside the broken SUV. The same car that had caused their death was now their last refuge.

As soon as they got inside, they heard something scurrying in the darkness outside.

Thap-thap-thap-thap.

From all sides.

The ghost was no longer alone.

In the darkness, the four of them huddled together. The car's windows were smashed, so the cold, putrid air from outside was pouring straight in.

"Where is she?" Priya whispered. Her voice was still trembling. The burnt marks on her neck were still fresh, but strangely, they weren't burning. There was just a cold sensation.

“She’s still here” Meera said softly. “She’s right here. In the darkness.”

Rahul, who was now in the driver’s seat (because Karan was still numb with shock in the passenger seat), gripped the steering wheel tightly.

“We have to leave”, Rahul said, grinding his teeth. “We’ll die sitting here.”

“Car is dead, Rahul”, Karan said in a dead voice. “Battery is dead. The engine is cold.”

To hell with logic! Rahul yelled. His fear had now turned to rage. “I won’t let us die here!”

Rahul slammed his palm on the Start button.

VROOOOOOM!

Everyone was startled.

The engine started in a single jerk. No sputtering, no hesitation. It was as if the car had been waiting for this very moment. The dashboard lights flickered on—but they weren’t normal blue. They were red. Speedometer, tachometer, fuel gauge… everything glowed a blood-like red.

Headlights blazed on. Two powerful beams tore through the intense darkness ahead.

“I told you guys!” Rahul laughed like a madman. “It started! See, Karan? It started!”

Without losing a second, Rahul shifted gears and pressed his foot on the accelerator.

The SUV jolted and lunged forward. The tyres gripped the concrete, and the car sped away.

20…

40…

60…

80 km/hr.

The wind rushed in through the broken windows, whipping their hair. The noise was deafening, but they liked this noise. This was the noise of 'life'. The noise of escape.

"Go Rahul! Speed Up!" Priya screamed, turning back repeatedly to check if that woman was following them.

Rahul increased the speed even more. 100 km/hr.

The tunnel's lights (which were now back on, but flickering eerily) rapidly fell behind.

Whoosh… Whoosh… Whoosh…

"Almost there", Rahul said, his eyes fixed on the road. "Bhatan Tunnel is only 1.5 km long. At 100 speed, we should be out in 1 minute."

Karan glanced at the dashboard clock. The time was stuck: 2:17 AM.

One minute passed.

Two minutes passed.

The car was racing at full speed. The engine was screaming. But the tunnel's exit was nowhere in sight.

Three minutes.

"Where's the exit?" Priya asked nervously. "We should have been out by now."

"Coming anytime" Rahul reassured himself. "Maybe we can't see it because of the fog."

He increased his speed even more.

120 km/hr.

The road was the same. The same concrete walls. The same yellow lights. The same peeling paint.

Five minutes passed.

By now, they should have covered at least 8-10 kilometers. Bhatan Tunnel was only 1.5 km. No tunnel in the world was **this** long.

"Rahul, slow down!" Meera suddenly cried out. Her gaze was fixed on the side of the road.

"Shut up, Meera! I'm not stopping!" Rahul yelled.

"Rahul, look there!" Meera pointed.

On the left side of the road, a fire extinguisher box was mounted on the wall. The glass of the box was shattered, and 'HELP' was written on it in red.

"So what?" Rahul said. "It's a fire box."

"We just crossed this," Meera's voice was laced with terror. "Two minutes ago. I read 'HELP'."

"You've gone mad," Rahul refused to believe. "All boxes look the same."

But the very next moment, they saw it again.

Black skid marks of tires on the road. The same marks their car had made when it flipped over.

And there, on the side of the road… lay a broken side-view mirror. Their car's own mirror.

Karan's breath hitched. "This… this is the accident spot. We've come back to the same place."

"Impossible!" Rahul screamed, punching the steering wheel. "I didn't turn the car! I'm driving straight! Straight!"

"The road is curving, Rahul," Karan said softly, his face ghostly pale. "This road isn't straight. It's a circle. We're going round and round."

"No!" Rahul floored the accelerator. The speedometer hit 140. "I will finish this tunnel!"

The car seemed to be talking to the wind. The engine was no longer roaring, it was crying.

Ten minutes passed.

The same fire box.

The same tire marks.

The same broken mirror.

Again and again.

Continuously.

The faster they drove, the sooner they returned to the same spot.

"Stop it!" Priya began to cry. "Rahul, please stop! I'm feeling dizzy!"

Finally, Rahul's courage broke. He slowed the car and hit the brakes. The car stopped right back where they had started—at their 'accident spot'.

The engine didn't turn off, it just idled, like an animal breathing.

Silence fell once more.

But this time, it was a silence of defeat.

"We're trapped," Rahul slammed his head on the steering wheel. He was crying. "Why isn't the road ending?"

Just then, the radio switched on again.

This time there was no static. The voice was perfectly clear.

A little girl's voice: "Mummy, look… new toys have come."

And then the same woman's voice: "Yes, son. We'll play with them for a very long time. Forever."

All the tunnel lights went out simultaneously.

Only the car's headlights remained on, illuminating the endless darkness ahead.

Karan looked outside. Now shadows were moving on the tunnel walls. Thousands of shadows. As if the tunnel walls had come alive.

They were in the *Chakravyuh*. And like *Abhimanyu*, they had entered, but the way out was sealed.

5

The Journalist's Sin

The engine had stalled.

This time, Rahul had shut it off. When you realize you're running in a circle, there's no point in running anymore. Running only brings exhaustion, not freedom.

There was a deep silence inside the car. Outside, shadows on the tunnel walls were still dancing, but they weren't coming closer to the car. They just stood far away, waiting.

"We're going to die here," Rahul rested his head on the steering wheel. His voice was broken. The boy who always acted like a 'daredevil' now looked like a terrified child.

"Shut up," Karan said softly. He was sitting in the passenger seat, staring at the dashboard. "We're not going to die. We're missing something. Every puzzle has a solution."

"This isn't a puzzle, Karan!" Priya screamed, her fear now turning into anger. "This… this is black magic! This is a ghost! Your engineering logic won't work here!"

"Then what do we do?" Karan turned, madness in his eyes. "Sit here with folded hands? Wait for that woman to come and devour us?"

"Shhh…" Meera quieted them both.

Meera was sitting in the back seat. She wasn't fighting. She wasn't crying. She was just looking at her closed fist.

"Meera, what happened?" Priya asked.

"How did this get into my hand?" Meera opened her fist.

In her hand was a piece of paper. An old, yellowed piece of paper.

"What is this?" Karan asked and reached out to take the paper.

"I don't know," Meera said. "When we were driving… I felt something under the seat. I just picked it up."

Karan switched on his mobile's flashlight (which was still working, though there was no network) and shone the light on the paper.

It was a Photograph.

It was a black and white photo, but it had turned yellow with time. In the photo, there was a bride and a groom standing. The bride was very beautiful—the same long hair, the same big eyes they had seen in the tunnel. But in the photo, she was smiling. There was vitality in her smile, not death.

The groom was standing beside her, but someone had scratched out the groom's face with a blade. There was only a white mark there.

Karan flipped the photo. Something was written on the back with an ink pen.

"Shalini weds Vikram - 12th October 2018"

"Shalini…" Priya read the name, and her breath hitched.

"Do you know her?" Rahul immediately asked, seeing the color drain from Priya's face.

Priya didn't answer. Her eyes were fixated on that name. Shalini.

"Priya?" Karan grabbed her arm. "Do you know her?"

Priya shook her head, "No… how would I know her? She must be some random girl…"

"Liar!"

No one in the car made that sound.

The sound came from the photo.

The photo slipped from Karan's hand and fell.

The photo didn't fall to the ground; instead, it floated in the air.

"What the hell is this…" Rahul recoiled into his seat.

The photo flipped in the air.

And the bride in that photo—Shalini—turned her neck inside the photo itself and looked straight at Priya.

Photo-Shalini's lips moved, and a thin, radio-static-like voice echoed in the car:

"Remember the article, Priya? 'The Unfortunate Accident'?"

A scream escaped Priya's mouth and she covered her ears. "Stop it! Stop it!"

"Which article?" Karan shook Priya. "Priya, what is she saying? What are you hiding?"

Priya started crying. "I didn't do anything! It was just an accident! The editor told me to drop the story!"

"Story?" Meera leaned forward, there was a strange anger in her voice—as if it wasn't Meera, but someone else speaking. "That wasn't a story, Priya. That was my LIFE!"

Suddenly, there was a loud THUD on the car's roof.

The whole car shook.

The flashlight went out. Darkness fell.

And in the darkness, on the seat next to Priya—which had been empty until now—there was the sound of someone sitting down. A crrrreaaak sound of the leather seat sinking.

Priya held her breath. She felt someone's hair on her shoulder. Cold, wet hair.

A cold breath touched her ear.

"Tell them…" the voice whispered in Priya's ear. "Tell them how much you sold my blood for?

Priya's breath hitched in her throat. The weight of the "thing" sitting next to her pressed into the seat. Its cold breath on her ear was like an icy wind.

"Speak…" the voice came again. "Speak, or I'll rip out your tongue."

Priya burst into tears. "I'll tell you! I'll tell you everything! Please don't hit me!"

Karan shone his flashlight on Priya's face. In its beam, Priya's face was pale and wet with tears. "Priya, what have you done?" Karan demanded, a mix of anger and fear in his voice. "Who is this Shalini?"

Priya began to speak, her lips trembling.

"Two years ago… October 2018," Priya's voice faltered. "I was a crime reporter then. I got a tip late at night. There was an accident on the Expressway."

"I thought it would be a normal truck accident," Priya explained. "But when I got there… Police had the whole area blocked off. There was no truck there. There was a red Sports Car. It was a Ferrari, I think. Its bonnet was completely smashed."

Priya took a deep breath, as if the scene was replaying before her eyes.

"And by the side of the road… she was lying there. Shalini."

"She was in a bridal dress," Priya sobbed. "Her whole body was soaked in blood. The sindoor in her parting had mixed with her blood. The police were quickly putting her body into the ambulance, as if she were trash."

"So why didn't you report it?" Rahul asked. "That would have been breaking news."

"Because that car…" Priya looked down, ashamed. "That car belonged to MLA Deshmukh's son. He was drunk. He hit Shalini. Shalini was alone on the highway, asking for help… and he…"

Priya fell silent.

"Go on…" a voice came from the darkness.

Priya looked around, crying, she folded her hands in the air as if begging for forgiveness. "Forgive me, please!" Taking Priya's silence as a refusal, a loud, ear-splitting, furious roar was heard.

"Tell them I was alive."

Priya screamed in terror. "Yes! Yes! She was alive!"

Everyone went quiet.

"What?" Meera asked softly. "She was alive?"

"When the police picked her up," Priya said, crying, "She was still breathing. She was trying to say something. She was raising her hand. But…"

Priya buried her face in her hands.

"But the MLA's son was standing there. He handed a bundle of cash to the police inspector. He said, 'Don't take her to the hospital. Finish her off on the way'."

Karan and Rahul were dumbfounded.

"And what did you do?" Karan asked with disgust. "You saw this and did nothing?"

"I was scared, Karan!" Priya said defensively. "Those people were powerful! They saw me. The MLA's man told me that if I published that news, my career would be over. My life would be over."

Now there was the pain of truth in Priya's voice.

"They offered me fifty lakh."

And promotion to Senior Editor's post."

"And you took it?" Rahul asked.

Priya nodded yes. "Yes. I took it. I wrote in the report that it was a 'Hit and Run', unknown vehicle. I wrote that the girl came to the highway to commit suicide."

There was a deep silence inside the car. The storm outside seemed calm in the face of this truth.

"Suicide…" the voice came from the darkness. That voice was now filled with more pain than anger. "I was going to start a new life… My groom dropped me off the car after a fight and drove away… I was asking for a lift to go back home…"

Suddenly, the SUV car's dashboard light flickered on. Red light.

FORMATION

And next to Priya, she finally appeared.

Shalini.

She wasn't burnt completely. This time she looked just as she did at the time of her death. Her bridal dress was torn. Her legs were broken. One of her eyes was hanging out.

She bent very close to Priya.

"You killed me, Priya," Shalini said. "That car broke my bones. But you… you killed my soul. You changed my story."

Priya screamed "Please!" and tried to open the door. This time the door opened.

Priya fell out of the car, onto the road. She started trying to crawl away.

"Priya, stop!" Karan yelled and ran after her.

But Priya had gone mad. She was running ahead into the dark tunnel. "Let me go! I'll return the money! Forgive me!"

She kept running in the darkness.

Just then, two bright headlights lit up from the front.

From the darkness of the tunnel came the sound of a red Ferrari.

The engine's ROAR was like a hungry lion.

VROOOOOM!

Priya stopped in the middle of the road. She covered her eyes with her hands.

"No…" Priya whispered.

That Ferrari had materialized out of thin air. It wasn't a real car.

It was the ghost of Shalini's memories.

The Ferrari sped towards Priya.

"Priya, move!" Rahul and Karan shouted from behind.

But Priya didn't move. She just kept staring at the bright light.

THUD!

There was a loud crash.

But Priya didn't fly into the air. As soon as the Ferrari hit her, Priya vanished.

The Ferrari also turned into smoke.

The road was empty.

Only Priya's mobile phone lay on the road, its screen shattered and flashlight still on.

Karan and Rahul ran to the spot.

"Priya?" Karan looked around. "Priya!"

No one was there. No blood, no body.

Only Champa (Magnolia champaca) flowers were scattered on the road, near the mobile.

Meera, who was still standing by the car, slowly said:
"She took her. To complete her story."

6

The Separation

The silence after Priya vanished was like shattered glass, piercing the tunnel.

The road was empty. Where Priya had screamed just seconds ago, now there was only air. And those Champa flowers… which suddenly turned from white to black and scattered into ash in the wind.

"Priya!" Rahul yelled. His voice was ragged. "Priya, this isn't a joke! Come out!"

Rahul was frantically hitting the spot where Priya had fallen, as if she was pretending to be invisible. But his hands only met air and cold concrete.

Karan was still standing exactly where he had stopped. His mind had gone numb. He closed his eyes, then opened them again. Vanished.

How can a person disappear into thin air?

The laws of physics weren't working here.

Matter can neither be created nor destroyed—he had read that.

But here?

Here, people were being erased.

"She's gone, Rahul," Meera said softly. She was calm, but this calm was more dangerous than fear. It was the calm of acceptance.

"You shut up!" Rahul turned angrily towards Meera. He grabbed her collar. "This is all because of you! You've been spouting ominous things from the start! You know something, don't you? Tell me!"

"Rahul, leave her!" Karan intervened, pushing Rahul away. "Are you crazy? We're not enemies!"

Rahul stumbled backward, falling. He was panting, his eyes filled with both tears and rage. "Then where did she go? Tell me, Karan! What does your logic say now? Wormhole? Mass hallucination?"

Karan had no answer. He just lowered his head. "I don't know."

Just then, a voice came from the deep darkness of the tunnel.

"Help…"

It was Priya's voice.

The three of them were startled. The voice had come from further inside the tunnel.

"Priya?" Rahul immediately stood up.

"Rahul… Karan… I'm here…" The voice was agonizing, like someone speaking from deep inside a well. "It's dark… I can't see anything…"

"She's alive!" A ray of hope lit up Rahul's eyes. "She's ahead! Maybe a car hit her and threw her forward!"

"No, Rahul, stop," Meera warned. "That's not Priya."

"You want her to die, don't you?" Rahul glared at Meera and then started running towards the darkness. "Priya! I'm coming! Keep shouting, Priya!"

Karan looked at Meera. Meera shook her head no. "Karan, don't let him go. This is a trap. It wants to separate us."

But Karan's friend was running ahead. He couldn't leave him alone.

"Rahul, wait!" Karan ran after him too. Meera, out of compulsion, followed them.

The three of them were running in the dark. The tunnel lights were now completely off. Only the flashlight of Karan's mobile (which Rahul had) showed a moving path.

"I'm here…" The voice was now coming from even further away.

Rahul ran even faster. "Priya, we're coming!"

Suddenly, Rahul stopped.

The path had split into two.

This was impossible.

The Bhatan Tunnel is a straight tunnel. There are no turns, no diversions. But in front of them, the tunnel wall had split.

One path went straight.

The other path, inside the wall, looked like an ancient cave, from where the sound of dripping water was coming.

"Karan… Rahul…"

Priya's voice came from that cave-like path.

"She's inside," Rahul aimed his flashlight towards the cave. Something was glinting on the ground there. Priya's other earring.

"Rahul, don't go inside," Karan grabbed his arm. "This isn't part of the tunnel. This is something else."

"She's my friend, Karan!" Rahul yanked his hand free. "If I don't go inside, I'll never forgive myself."

Rahul, without a second thought, plunged into that dark, cave-like path.

"Rahul!" Karan yelled.

As soon as Rahul went inside, a strong gust of wind came.

WHOOSH!

And that 'cave' path… it closed.

The stone walls joined together. Where there had just been a path, now there was only a plain concrete wall.

"Rahul!" Karan punched the wall. "Rahul!"

No answer. No sound. Rahul had vanished behind that wall.

Karan, panting, turned around.

Now only he and Meera were left.

Meera was standing in the middle of the road, but she wasn't looking at Karan. She was looking at the tunnel's ceiling.

"Karan…" Meera whispered. "She's choosing us one by one. First 'Sinner' (Priya). Then 'Anger' (Rahul)."

Karan gripped Meera's shoulders. "So what do we do now? I don't understand anything?"

Meera slowly lowered her neck and looked into Karan's eyes.

"I am 'Belief', Karan. And you… you are 'Denial'."

Just then, from behind them, from where their car should have been, came the sound of a child crying.

Karan looked back.

The car was gone.

The tunnel was gone.

"Karan, look down!" Meera screamed.

Karan looked down. The road… the road wasn't concrete anymore. It had turned into black, filthy water.

Seconds ago, they were standing in the tunnel, but now they were on a broken bridge. All around them, furious water raged. The air reeked of mud and rotten fish.

"What kind of illusion is this?" Karan tried to pull his feet out of the water. The water was ice cold and had reached his knees. "Meera, let's get to higher ground!"

"This isn't an illusion, Karan!" Meera's face had gone white. Her eyes were fixed on the sky above, where the tunnel ceiling was gone and black clouds thundered. "These are her memories. She died right here. This is the bridge from which she…"

Suddenly, a large whirlpool formed in the water.

Meera's feet lost their grip. She slipped.

"Karan!" Meera reached out her hand.

Karan lunged and grabbed Meera's hand. "I've got you! I won't let you go!"

But the current was too strong. It wasn't ordinary water; it was heavy and sticky, like a mixture of blood and oil.

Meera's body was being dragged underwater.

"She's calling me…" Meera gasped, spitting out water. "She wants me to feel what it's like to drown."

"Don't talk nonsense!" Karan pulled with all his might. His muscles screamed in pain. "Meera, don't let go! Fight, Meera!"

But Meera's eyes rolled back. She wasn't looking at Karan anymore. She had gone into a trance.

"It's cold…" Meera's voice changed. It wasn't Meera's voice anymore. It was Shalini's voice—wet, heavy, and full of agony. "Can't breathe… Someone please save me…"

Karan was terrified. "Meera, come back!"

Black hands emerged from the water. Thousands of hands. Rotten fingers. They grabbed Meera's feet, gripped her waist, and started pulling her down.

"NO!" Karan screamed.

With a violent jerk, Meera's hand slipped from Karan's grasp.

SPLASH!

Meera vanished into the black water.

"Meeraaaaa!"

Karan thrashed in the water, trying to find her. But there was no water there.

The moment Meera disappeared, the illusion of the "Bridge" and "Water" shattered.

Karan fell back onto the dry, concrete road of Bhatan Tunnel. His face hit the ground.

There was no water. No bridge.

He was alone. In the dark tunnel.

"Meera?" Karan called out. His voice trembled. "Rahul? Priya?"

No answer. Only the whispering 'sann-sann' sound of the tunnel's wind.

He was left alone. His logic, his friends, his strength—everything had been snatched away.

[Scene Shift: Rahul]

Meanwhile, where was Rahul?

When he heard Priya's voice and entered that cave, and the path closed off, he kept running in the dark.

"Priya! I'm here!" Rahul shouted.

But after going a little distance, the path started becoming narrow.

First, he could walk standing up.

Then he had to bend down.

Then he had to crawl on his knees.

Now he was stuck in a pipe-like space. All around were concrete walls pressing against his body. Oxygen in the air was low.

“Where have I ended up?” Rahul tried to turn back.

But he couldn’t turn. There was so little space that he couldn’t even move.

“Karan! Help!” Rahul screamed. His voice just echoed within itself.

In the dark, he took out a lighter from his pocket. (Rahul was a smoker, he always kept a lighter with him).

Click. Phusss.

A small flame ignited.

In that dim light, Rahul saw where he was.

He wasn’t in some pipe.

He was in Shalini’s Big coffin.

On the walls were scratches from fingernails. Thousands of marks. And among those marks, something was written in blood:

“HELP ME”

“LET ME OUT”

“I AM ALIVE”

Rahul started choking. “No… no…”

Just then, a sound came from near his feet.

Khurrr… Khurrr…

As if someone was crawling towards him in that narrow space.

Rahul aimed the lighter in that direction.

From the darkness, a burnt face emerged.

Shalini.

She was crawling upside down, like a chipkali (lizard). Her neck was twisted at a broken angle, but her eyes were fixed on Rahul.

"Not enough space, is there?" Shalini whispered. "Imagine how it felt for me when they buried me alive?"

Rahul screamed, but there was no air to scream with.

Shalini extended her hand and snatched the lighter's flame.

Phusss.

The fire went out.

Now there was only darkness. And Rahul's screams.

[Scene Shift: Karan]

Back in the tunnel, Karan was still sitting on the ground.

From far away…

Very far away…

He heard Rahul's screams. The sound was coming from inside the walls of the tunnel.

"Rahul!" Karan ran towards the wall and started hitting it. "I can hear you! Rahul!"

But the sound slowly faded and then stopped.

Karan, exhausted, slumped against the wall. He was utterly broken.

"Why are you doing this?" Karan asked into the dark. He was crying. "What have we done? We just came for a drive!"

From the front, in the darkness, a Candle lit up.

Then another.

Then a third.

In no time, thousands of candles lit up in the middle of the road.

In the light of those candles, a pyre became visible. A heap of wood.

And on top of that pyre… Meera was lying.

She was unconscious (or perhaps dead). And around her, fire was about to ignite.

Karan stood up. This was the last chance.

"Meera!"

He ran towards the fire.

7

The Visions

The tunnel was no longer a tunnel. It had transformed into a crematorium.

Thousands of candles burned in the middle of the road. In their light, that pile of wood — a pyre — looked like a black mountain. And on top of that pile, Meera lay.

She was unconscious. Her hands and feet weren't tied with rope, yet she wasn't moving. As if someone had ripped her soul from her body.

"Meera!" Karan screamed.

He was running. Running with all his might. But just like in dreams, the faster he tried to run, the farther the destination seemed. The air had grown thick, sticky like honey, holding him back.

As he got closer to the pyre, the temperature began to rise.

Until now, there had been an icy cold in the tunnel. But now? Now a heatwave was blowing through. Karan's skin began to burn. Sweat ran down his forehead and into his eyes.

And then he saw them.

Three shadows stood around the pyre.

They weren't human. They were figures made of smoke. Their faces were hazy, but their movements were human-like.

One shadow was emptying a large can over the pyre.

Gug-gug-gug…

A sharp, foul smell assailed Karan's nostrils. This wasn't the scent of jasmine.

This was the smell of Petrol.

"Stop!" Karan shrieked. "Leave her! She's alive!"

Karan lunged forward and tried to push the shadow that was pouring the petrol.

SWISH!

Karan's hand passed right through the shadow. As if he were punching the air. Karan lost his balance and fell near the pile of wood.

The shadow didn't stop. It continued to pour the petrol. The liquid that was falling was soaking Meera's clothes.

Karan tried to grab Meera's foot to pull her away.

Zzzzt!

The moment he touched Meera, he felt an electric shock. Karan recoiled with a jolt. His fingers went numb.

"You can't save her," a deep male voice said.

Karan looked up, startled. This voice hadn't come from those shadows. This voice was in the air of the tunnel.

"Who's speaking?" Karan snarled, in pain and anger.

Another shadow came forward. In this shadow's hand was a matchbox.

Karan saw that the shadow was saying something. Although it had no face, the words echoed directly in Karan's mind. It was like Telepathy — he was hearing the voices of the past.

"Burn her," the voice came into Karan's mind. "The evidence will be destroyed. The police will think the car caught fire after the accident."

Karan understood. He wasn't seeing a ghost. He was witnessing a replay of Shalini's death.

These were the people — the MLA's son and his friends. Instead of taking Shalini to the hospital, they had decided to burn her alive so that the accident would look like a "mishap".

"No…" Karan whispered. "These people are animals…"

The shadow pulled out a matchstick.

Kharrr…

A small spark ignited.

That yellow flame looked incredibly dangerous in the darkness.

"MEERA, WAKE UP!" Karan screamed with all his might. "IT'S ABOUT TO CATCH FIRE!"

But Meera didn't move. Drops of petrol were dripping from her face.

The shadow tossed the burning matchstick into the air.

Karan watched the matchstick fall in slow-motion. It spun as it came down… straight towards Meera's petrol-soaked clothes.

Without thinking, without caring about the shock, Karan put his hand in between.

He wanted to catch that matchstick.

But that matchstick passed right through his hand. It wasn't a real matchstick. It was a memory.

That matchstick fell on Meera (Shalini).

FWOOOM!

With an explosion, fire erupted.

The flames rose 10 feet into the air. The heat was so intense that the tips of Karan's hair singed. He was forced to step back.

And then… the screams began.

It was Meera's voice. But that scream wasn't Meera's. It was so painful that it felt as if someone's soul was being squeezed dry.

"IT'S BURNING! EVERYTHING IS BURNING!"

Karan covered his face with his hand, to protect himself from the heat of the fire. "Stop it! Stop this! She'll die!"

He picked up the dirt lying on the ground and tried to throw it on the fire. Useless.

In the middle of the fire, Meera's body had stiffened. She was writhing in agony.

Karan, who always relied on logic and science, was utterly helpless for the first time today. Science had no formula to change the past.

He did what a defeated man does.

He fell to his knees, joined his hands, and yelled:

"FORGIVE US! FORGIVE US!

"FORGIVE ME!" Karan's scream was swallowed by the roar of the flames.

But that fire… it was strange. It was touching Meera's body, blackening her clothes, but not turning them to ash. This fire wasn't burning the body; it was burning the soul.

Suddenly, the faces of the three shadows standing around the fire began to clear. The smoke cleared, and Karan recognized them.

They weren't ghosts. They were humans.

The middle boy—the one who had thrown the match—was Vikram Deshmukh. The same MLA's son Priya had told him about. He was wearing an expensive leather jacket and held a bottle of alcohol in his hand. He was laughing. There was cruelty in his laugh.

"Let the bitch burn," Vikram shouted. "By tomorrow morning, only bones will be left. No evidence."

The second boy, who looked a little scared, said, "Bro, what if someone sees us?"

"Who's gonna see?" Vikram pointed towards the road. "This is Bhatan Tunnel. Everyone drives through here blind. No one stops."

Karan was stunned to hear this.

No one stops.

That's exactly what they had done. When the driver at the dhaba warned them, they didn't stop. When Priya saw the accident, she didn't stop. The world keeps moving at its own pace, and girls like Shalini burn to ashes on the roadside.

"We're watching!" Karan screamed, though he knew this was the past and they couldn't hear him. "We're watching, Vikram! We're watching your sin!"

As soon as Karan admitted this, the color of the fire changed.

The yellow fire now turned blue and black.

Meera, who had been screaming until now, suddenly fell silent. She opened her eyes from within the flames.

Her eyes were no longer Meera's brown eyes. They were black. Her entire eyeball was black.

Meera (or Shalini within her) sat up. Fire danced around her.

She looked directly at Karan and spoke in a voice that was not human:

"They burned me… so the truth would be hidden. But ash… ash never lies, Karan."

BOOM!

There was a powerful explosion, as if the air pressure had increased.

All the candles blew out.

The pyre disappeared.

Vikram and his friends dissolved into the smoke.

The flames vanished.

Silence returned.

The cold, concrete road of Bhatan Tunnel returned.

Karan was gasping, sprawled on the ground. His body was drenched in sweat.

"Meera?" Karan called out in the darkness.

A little distance away, someone was lying on the ground.

Karan crawled on his knees, reached her, and turned on his flashlight.

Meera was lying there. She was unconscious.

But she wasn't burned. Her clothes were intact. Not even her hair was singed.

But… there were black soot marks on her skin. As if someone had rubbed her with coal. And the smell of burnt flesh still hung fresh in the entire tunnel.

"Meera, please wake up," Karan placed her head in his lap and patted her cheeks. "Meera!"

Meera slowly opened her eyes.

Her eyes were back to normal, but a deep exhaustion pulled at them.

"Karan…" Meera said in a hoarse voice. "It's… it's burning so much."

"I know," Karan cried. "I know. But you survived. All that was fake. It was just a vision."

Meera grabbed Karan's hand. His hand was hot—feverishly hot.

"It wasn't fake, Karan," Meera whispered. "I felt that pain. When skin melts… when breath stops… I felt it all."

Meera tried to get up but fell. "She wants us to understand. Not just to see, but to understand."

Karan helped her up and leaned her against the wall. "We understood, Meera. Priya took money. Rahul ignored. I made fun. We are all guilty."

"Rahul…" Meera said his name. "Where is Rahul?"

Karan's heart sank. He had completely forgotten.

"He… he was left behind that wall," Karan gestured towards where the path had been blocked.

But when Karan shone the torch in that direction, there was no blocked path.

The tunnel was straight. The wall was plain.

But something was lying on the ground there.

Karan slowly walked over.

It was Rahul's shoe.

And near that shoe, on the concrete, something was written. Not with blood. But someone had scratched the concrete with their nails to write:

SORRY

Karan picked up the shoe. It was empty. Rahul had vanished.

"She took him," Meera said from behind. Her voice was flat now. "Priya is gone. Rahul is gone. Now it's just us."

Karan held the shoe to his chest and for the first time—perhaps in years—he broke down and cried. That engineer, that project manager, that logical man… today he had lost.

"Whyyyyy?"

Karan screamed, looking up at the ceiling.

"Rahul was just driving! What wrong did he do to anyone?"

No answer came from the darkness. Just the whooshing sound of the wind seemed to say: "To be ignorant is also a sin."

Meera stood, leaning against the wall. "This isn't the time to cry, Karan. If we want to save our souls… then we have to finish this story."

"How?" Karan asked, wiping his tears. "We can't escape by car. We can't escape on foot either. What do we do?"

Meera put her hand in her pocket and pulled something out.

It was the packet of incense sticks she had brought in the car at the beginning, for a 'shubh shuruwat' (Happy Beginning).

"We have to apologize," Meera said. "But not just by speaking. We have to bring her liberation."

8

The Breakdown

Karan was still sitting on the ground, holding Rahul's empty shoe in his hand.

An eerie silence filled the tunnel. That noise, that fire, those screams—everything was gone. But the noise in Karan's mind was still deafening. Thousands of questions, thousands of accusations.

"It's all my fault," Karan whispered, his voice trembling. "If I had stopped at that dhaba… if I had listened to Meera… if I had stopped Rahul…"

Meera came to him and put her hand on his shoulder. "Karan, this isn't the time for regret. We have to move forward."

Karan angrily shook Meera's hand off. "Forward? Where forward, Meera? The road is blocked! We're going in circles! Priya is dead, Rahul is dead. Now we're just waiting for our own turn."

Karan stood up and screamed into the darkness of the tunnel. "Take me too! End this game!"

Just then… he heard a voice.

"Brother…"

Karan stopped. This voice… It was Rahul's voice.

"Brother, why did you leave me behind?"

Karan looked around. “Rahul? Where are you?”

Meera grabbed Karan. “Karan, that’s not Rahul. It’s playing with your mind.”

“No! It’s Rahul!” Karan pushed Meera away and ran in the direction from which the voice had come.

A shadow appeared on the tunnel wall. It looked like Rahul. It was limping, as if its leg was broken.

“You said you’d take care of it,” the Shadow said, its voice filled with pain and anger. “You said, ‘I’ll drive, we’ll be safe.’ Look how safe we are.”

“Forgive me, buddy!” Karan cried, moving towards the shadow. “I didn’t do it on purpose.”

The Shadow turned around.

When it showed its face, Karan screamed.

It was Rahul… but Rahul after the crash. His head was smashed (which wasn’t visible before) from hitting the dashboard. One of his eyes hung out. His jaw was broken.

“You were wearing your seatbelt, Karan,” Ghost-Rahul said, spitting blood. “You saved yourself. And you let me die.”

“No! I tried!” Karan started backing away.

Now Priya’s voice came from the other side of the tunnel.

“Fifty lakhs, Karan,” Priya’s voice echoed. “I took the money, yes. But what did you do? You refused to even hear the truth. Your ‘Logic’ turned out to be more dangerous than my greed.”

Karan fell to his knees and covered his ears. “Stop it! Stop these voices!”

But the voices didn’t stop. They grew louder.

“Killer…”

“Coward…”

"Fraud…"

From every wall, every corner of the tunnel, these words rained down on Karan like stones. Karan's mind was about to explode. He started banging his head on the ground like a madman. "Quiet! Quiet! Quiet!"

Meera ran to him. She held Karan's head to prevent him from hurting himself.

"Karan, look into my eyes!" Meera screamed.

Karan opened his eyes. They were red, filled with madness.

"This isn't real," Meera said sternly. "Rahul isn't blaming you. This is Shalini."

"She is using your 'Guilt' to break you. If you break, she wins."

"I'm already broken, Meera!" Karan cried. "I can't fight anymore."

Meera slapped Karan hard across his cheek.

SLAP!

A deafening silence fell upon the tunnel. Karan fell silent, staring at Meera in shock.

"You **have** to fight," Meera said angrily, tears welling in her eyes. "For Rahul. For Priya. They will only find peace when we break this curse. If we lose, they will wander in this tunnel forever. Do you want Rahul to suffer this pain endlessly?"

Karan remembered Rahul's shattered ghost.

"No," Karan said softly. "No, I won't let that happen."

Meera extended her hand. "Then stand up. We have to talk to her. No more running. No more hiding. Now, we will confront her."

Karan took Meera's hand and stood up. He took a deep breath and silenced the storm in his mind.

"Where is she?" Karan asked, his voice now devoid of fear, replaced by a weary courage.

Meera gestured towards the middle of the road.

There, smoke was gathering in the air. That smoke was slowly taking shape.

Shalini was returning. But this time she wasn't coming to scare them. She was coming for their answer.

The smoke had now fully taken on a human form.

Shalini stood there. In the middle of the road.

This time she wasn't burnt. Her face was clear, beautiful, just a pale color. She wore a red wedding dress, stained with blood and mud. Her eyes were no longer black, but held a deep, infinite sorrow.

She didn't look like a terrifying ghost, but rather a defeated bride.

Karan and Meera stood before her. Fear was still there, but now that fear wasn't stopping them.

"Shalini…" Meera slowly spoke her name.

The woman turned her neck. "You know my name…" her voice came like a whisper in the wind.

"We know everything," Meera bravely took a step forward. In her hand was that packet of incense sticks. "We know what happened to you. Vikram… that accident… that fire. We saw everything."

Anger began to appear on Shalini's face. "Saw? Yes… you all just watch. That night too, people watched. Cars kept passing by. No one stopped. Everyone thought, 'it's someone else's problem'."

The wind picked up. The tunnel lights began to flicker again.

"You are all the same," Shalini screamed.

"Selfish.

Cowards."

"Yes!" Karan stepped forward. "Yes, we are selfish! We are cowards!"

Shalini stopped, a little surprised by Karan's admission.

Tears streamed down Karan's eyes. "We were lost in our own world. We thought we were safe because we hadn't done anything wrong. But you're right… doing nothing is also a sin."

Karan knelt down.

"But no more," Karan said. "We know your story now. Priya… Priya made a mistake, but she wanted to regret it. Rahul… he was just naive. Leave them, Shalini. Punish us. I am ready."

Shalini came close to Karan. She leaned in and looked at Karan's face.

"You want to die?" she asked.

"I want to give you freedom," Karan said. "We cannot give you justice. Vikram and those people… they might have escaped. But we promise… if we get out of here, we will tell the whole world what happened in this tunnel. Your name won't be 'Ghost', it will be 'Shalini'."

Meera quickly pulled out a lighter and lit the incense stick.

Phusss…

A faint smoke rose. That fragrance… the sacred fragrance of sandalwood and jasmine… began to cut through the stench of rotten champak and burnt flesh.

Meera joined her hands and closed her eyes. She wasn't chanting any mantra, just praying from the heart.

"Om Shanti…" Meera whispered. "Give her peace, God. Take her to you. End her pain."

The incense smoke began to swirl around Shalini.

Shalini was watching that smoke. Tears of blood began to flow from her eyes.

"Peace…" Shalini repeated the word, as if remembering something long forgotten. "I don't want peace. I want my groom. I want the life they snatched from me."

"It can't come back, Shalini," Meera cried. "What's gone is gone. You're trapped here. In pain. Do you want to stay like this forever? Amongst these stones? In this darkness?"

Shalini looked at the tunnel. That infinite darkness.

For a moment, she didn't look like a ghost, but just a 22-year-old girl who wanted to go home.

"If I let you go…" Shalini laid down a condition, "Will you truly tell my story?"

"I swear," Karan said. "I'll dedicate my whole life to it."

Shalini took a deep breath (or whatever she was capable of).

"Truth sets us free," Shalini said.

As soon as she uttered these words, a strong wind swept through the tunnel.

WHOOOOSH!

The incense stick in Meera's hand blew out.

But ahead in the tunnel… that deep darkness… began to crack.

From within the darkness, a White Light appeared. It was like sunlight. It was like the first ray of dawn.

"Go…" Shalini said. "Before my anger returns."

Karan and Meera looked at each other.

"Rahul?" Karan asked. "And Priya?"

Shalini gestured behind her.

There, by the roadside, Rahul and Priya lay unconscious.

“Rahul! Priya!” Karan ran towards them.

They lifted Rahul and Priya. Both were unconscious, but breathing.

“Hurry, Karan!” Meera urged. “We need to get to the car!”

But the car… it had vanished, hadn’t it?

No.

As soon as the light appeared, the SUV was visible again. It was badly damaged, but it was there.

“Let’s go!” Karan hoisted Rahul onto his shoulder and put him in the car’s backseat. Meera handled Priya.

He sat in the driver’s seat. He pressed the start button.

The Engine… Started.

Karan took one last look at Shalini. She was still standing there, dissolving into smoke. She waved her hand—not to say goodbye, but to shoo them away.

“Thank you,” Karan whispered and pressed the accelerator.

The car sped towards that white light which looked like the tunnel’s exit.

Karan was crying, tears of joy. “We’re saved, Meera! We’re saved!”

Meera was also smiling. “Truth sets us free, Karan.”

The light came closer.

The car entered that light.

Everything turned white.

Peace.

Tranquility.

Freedom.

Or… perhaps that's what they thought.

9

The False Exit

That white light slowly faded.

Karan had his eyes tightly shut, waiting for impact. But there was no impact. No sound.

Only the air changed.

The air that was previously rotten, stale, and suffocating… suddenly became fresh. It carried the scent of earth, of wet soil after the rain. There was a coolness, but it wasn't the coolness of death—this was the pleasant chill of a Western Ghaats morning.

"Karan…" Meera's voice came. It was trembling with happiness. "Open your eyes."

Karan hesitantly opened one eye.

In front of him, there were no dark concrete walls,

no flickering sodium lights,

no ghost.

Only a lush green mountain.

The SUV was driving on a smooth road. The first light of dawn was spreading across the sky—light blue and pink hues painting the clouds. Far away, the sun was trying to emerge from between the mountains.

"We… we're out?" Karan touched the steering wheel. This wasn't a dream. It was real.

"We're out!" Karan shouted loudly. "We're alive! Meera, we're alive!"

Karan slammed on the brakes and stopped the car by the roadside. He opened the door and leaped out.

He fell to the road and began to kiss the ground. "Thank you God! Thank you Shalini! Thank you!"

Meera also got out. She leaned against the car, taking deep breaths. Tears streamed from her eyes, but they were tears of joy.

There was a stir in the back seat.

Rahul and Priya, who were unconscious, were now regaining consciousness.

"My head…" Rahul groaned as he opened his eyes. "What happened? Have we arrived?"

Karan ran to the back and opened the door. "Rahul! Get up, man! We made it! We're out of the tunnel!"

Rahul stumbled out. He looked around—green valleys, the chirping of birds, and cool air.

"That… that woman…" Rahul asked, agitated. "Where is she?"

"She's gone," Meera said with a smile. "We set her free. She let us go."

Priya also came out. She was still in shock. She touched her neck where the ghost had held her. There was no mark there now.

"My marks are gone," Priya said in surprise. "My pain is also gone."

"It's all over, Priya," Karan hugged her. "It was a bad dream. Just a bad dream."

The four friends stood there by the roadside, watching the sun rising. This sight seemed to them the most beautiful sight in the world.

"What time is it?" Rahul asked.

Karan checked his wrist-watch.

6:15 AM.

"It's six o'clock," Karan said. "We were in that tunnel all night. Four hours."

"I thought we were there for years," Meera said softly.

Karan turned towards the car. His gaze fell upon the SUV.

There was something strange.

Inside the tunnel, the car was badly damaged. The windows were broken, the body was dented, the bumper was hanging.

But now?

In the sunlight, the Dark Blue SUV was gleaming.

The windshield was perfectly clean.

There was no dent.

There was no scratch.

Even the tyres looked new.

"The car…" Karan ran his hand over the car. "How did the car get fixed?"

"Maybe the damage wasn't as bad as we thought," Rahul reasoned, willing to believe anything in his joy. "It probably looked worse in the dark last night. Dude, this is a top model, its body is strong."

Karan couldn't swallow that logic. He himself had seen the shattered glass. But at that moment, he didn't want to ask questions. He just wanted to live in the moment.

"Let's go," Karan said. "Let's get out of here. Lonavala is close by. We'll stop there for hot tea and then head straight home. I don't want to stay on this highway for another second."

"Agreed," Priya said. "I just want to get to my bed."

Everyone got back into the car. The mood had lightened.

Rahul switched on the music system.

This time there was no static. No crying sound.

A cheerful RJ's voice came on FM: "Good Morning Mumbai! The weather is pleasant and you're listening to Radio Mirchi…"

Then an upbeat song started playing: *"Zindagi ek safar hai suhana…"*

Rahul laughed. "See? Everything's normal."

Karan put the car in gear and drove forward.

The wind blew in through the windows. Everything seemed normal.

But Meera… Meera was still looking back in the side-view mirror.

The road was empty.

There should have been traffic so early in the morning. Milk vans, newspapers trucks, buses.

But there was no one else on the road besides them.

"Karan," Meera said softly. "Where's the traffic?"

"It's early morning, Meera," Karan brushed it off. "And anyway, isn't it good that there's no traffic? We'll reach home quickly."

Meera went quiet. She thought she was overthinking. She just wanted to be happy.

But when Karan took a turn, Meera's gaze fell on the Distance Marker.

The stone read:

MUMBAI: 0 KM

Meera rubbed her eyes and looked again.

The stone was left behind.

"Zero kilometer?" Meera wondered. "We're going towards Pune. How can Mumbai be 0?"

She didn't say anything. She didn't want to call back the fear.

The car just kept going, in that golden light... which perhaps wasn't the light of the real sun.

The car was cruising smoothly on the highway, like butter. The sun was a bit higher now, and the heat was getting intense.

"I'm hungry, man," Rahul rubbed his stomach. "It'll take time to reach Lonavala. Let's eat something first."

Karan looked at the road ahead. "I see a Dhaba up ahead."

On the left side of the road, there was a big board. Written in yellow and red paint was:

SHER-E-PUNJAB DHABA

"Oh, that's the same name," Priya noted. "Where we stopped last night?"

"Must be a franchise," Rahul said casually. "There are a thousand dhabas named Sher-e-Punjab in India. Stop, Karan, their tea was good."

Karan turned the car onto the service road and parked it in front of the dhaba.

Everything seemed normal. The same charpais (khatiyas), the same smoke rising from the tandoor, the same line of trucks.

The four of them got out of the car and went to sit at an empty table.

"Bhaiya!" Rahul yelled. "Four masala chai and two plates of Aloo Paratha! With extra butter!"

A waiter, wearing a dirty kurta-pyjama, came towards their table. He had his head bowed, so his face wasn't clearly visible. He quietly wrote down the order (or pretended to) and left.

"Isn't this beautiful?" Priya took a long breath. "Normal life."

"I'm going to resign on Monday itself," Karan said, drumming his fingers on the table. "Enough of corporate stress. I'll do something simple. Maybe farming."

Everyone laughed. These were the promises people make after escaping death.

Just then, the waiter brought the tea.

He placed four glasses on the table. Steam was rising from the tea.

"Aaah," Rahul picked up a glass. "The real joy of life."

Rahul brought the glass to his mouth and took a big gulp.

Suddenly, Rahul's face changed. He immediately spat the tea back out.

THUU!

"What happened?" Karan asked.

Rahul was coughing. "What… what is this?"

He slammed the glass on the table.

It wasn't tea. Inside the glass was black, thick oil. And it wasn't tea leaves floating in it. Dead insects were floating in it.

"Ew!" Priya checked her glass.

There was no oil in her glass. Her glass was filled with ash. Dry, grey ash.

"Is this a joke?" Karan stood up angrily. "Waiter! Come here!"

But the waiter was gone.

Karan looked around.

Now he started noticing something strange in the dhaba.

People were sitting there—truck drivers, families. But no one was speaking.

Pin-drop silence.

They were just sitting, like statues. They had food in their hands, but no one was eating.

“Hello?” Karan went to a truck driver. The same old driver who had warned them last night.

“Baba?” Karan placed a hand on his shoulder.

The driver slowly turned.

His face… was flat.

No eyes, no nose, no mouth.

Just skin. A smooth, blank canvas.

“AAAHH!” Karan fell back.

Meera screamed. She saw that all the other people—those families, those children—their faces were gone. They weren’t humans. They were just mannequins.

The sun that was shining in the sky suddenly started flickering.

Zzzzt… Zzzzt…

The sun went out. Then it lit up again. Then it went out.

“The sun is flickering…” Meera said, looking up, terror in her voice. “This isn’t the sun.”

The moment the ‘Sun’ went out, a ceiling appeared above. A concrete ceiling.

They weren’t under the open sky. They were still inside the Bhatan Tunnel. That ‘Sun’ was a powerful Halogen Light in the tunnel. Those ‘Mountains’ were painted walls of the tunnel.

That ‘Dhaba’ was just a hallucination in their minds. The world turned dark again.

The table, chairs, food—everything turned into smoke.

The four of them were standing back on the road. Their car was back in its broken state.

And in front… a short distance away… lay that same Fire Box and that same broken mirror.

“We never went outside,” Karan knelt on the ground. “We’re still here. We’re still right here.”

Rahul started crying. “I drank tea… I tasted it… How can this be a lie?”

Just then, that voice echoed in the air. This time it wasn’t Shalini’s voice. It was a mixture of many voices—Shalini, Vikram, Harpal (the truck driver), and thousands of other people.

“Hope is the worst punishment,” the voice said. “Now you are broken.”

Karan picked up a stone from the road and tried to hit himself on the head. “End it! End me!”

Meera grabbed his hand.

“No, Karan,” Meera said. Her eyes were now completely dry. “That’s what she wants. For us to give up. For us to go crazy.”

“Then what else should we do?” Karan screamed. “We’re trapped, Meera! For eternity!”

Meera looked towards the car.

“We have to see the truth,” Meera said. “The real truth. The one we’re ignoring.”

“Which truth?”

“Whether we are alive or not,” Meera said. “We need to find the Wreckage. The wreckage of our car.”

“But we have the car!” Priya pointed to the broken SUV.

“This is the car in which our souls are trapped,” Meera explained. “But where are our bodies?”

Silence.

If they are ghosts, then their bodies must be lying somewhere.

"If we find our bodies," Meera said, "Then maybe we can break this loop. We have to accept our death."

Karan stood up. This was their last hope. "Come on," Karan said. "Let's go find our corpses."

10

The Wreckage

“Leave the car,” Meera said. “This car will take us where *it* wants to go, not where *we* need to be.”

Karan looked at the battered SUV. It was wrecked again, but the engine was still running. He turned it off.

Click.

Silence.

The four of them—Karan, Meera, Rahul, and Priya—now stood on the road. On foot.

“What do we need to find?” Rahul asked, all hope drained from his voice.

“We need to find Zero Point,” Karan said. “The place where we crashed. The real place.”

They started walking.

The darkness in the tunnel was deep, but their eyes had now adjusted to this gloom. They didn’t need a torch. Their bodies themselves emitted a faint blue glow—perhaps proof that they were no longer part of this world.

After walking for a while, Priya stopped.

“What’s this?” she picked something up from the ground.

It was a pair of Sunglasses. Rahul’s expensive aviator sunglasses.

But they were broken. The frame was bent and the glass was stained with blood.

"These are mine," Rahul said in surprise and checked his pocket.

He had the same sunglasses in his pocket—perfectly intact.

"Two sunglasses?" Rahul compared the two. "How is this possible?"

"The ones in your pocket, that's your 'memory'," Meera explained. "What's on the ground… that's 'reality'."

Rahul dropped the broken sunglasses right there, as if they were a hot coal.

They moved on.

A little further, they found more things.

A Shoe. Priya's high heel sandal. Its heel was broken and it lay on the road as if someone had abandoned it while fleeing.

A Watch. Karan's wrist-watch.

Karan picked it up. The dial was broken. The hands were stopped.

Time: 2:17 AM.

"This is the same time," Karan whispered. "When we entered the tunnel."

Slowly, the debris on the road began to increase.

First, there were small things. Then car parts started appearing.

A broken Bumper.

Thousands of shards of glass scattered on the road like diamonds.

A Number Plate that read: MH 02 ….

"We're close," Karan said. His heart (if it was still beating) was pounding hard.

The smell in the air had changed. It was no longer the stench of rotten Champa.

Now it was the smell of Petrol, Burnt Tyres, and… Flesh. The smell of raw, fresh death.

Priya covered her nose. "I can't go any further, Karan. This smell… I can't bear it."

"Just a little more, Priya," Karan held her hand. "We have to see it."

They took a few more steps.

And then… they saw it.

Under the tunnel's sodium lights, in the middle of the road, lay a crushed heap of iron.

It was Karan's SUV.

But it wasn't the same as the one they had just been driving.

This car was completely flattened.

The roof had merged with the seats.

The bonnet was crumpled like an accordion.

The car was upside down.

A pool of blood had spread everywhere. That blood had now dried and turned black.

"Oh my god…" Rahul fell to his knees.

The four of them went near the wreckage. There was fear, but also a strange attraction.

Karan bent down and peered inside through the broken window.

It was dark inside, but he could see.

On the driver's seat… there was someone.

On the passenger's seat… there was someone.

On the back seats… there were two people.

Karan held his breath.

"Meera..." Karan whispered. "We found our bodies."

But the bodies inside weren't just 'dead'. They were terribly mangled.

The body on the driver's seat (Karan's) had its head crushed into the steering wheel.

On the passenger's seat (Rahul's body), his face was unrecognizable.

In the back... Priya's body was hanging out of the broken glass.

And Meera?

Meera's body was stuck in the middle, hands clasped together, as if she was praying at the moment of her death.

Karan (the spirit) looked at Karan (the corpse).

This was the moment when 'Denial' completely shattered.

"We're dead," Karan said. This time there was no question. No hope. Just a cold, hard truth. "We died the moment the car flipped. At 2:17 AM."

Priya started crying loudly. "I didn't want to die! I wasn't even married yet! I had dreams!"

Rahul was just silent, looking at his corpse. "At least... it wouldn't have hurt," he falsely reassured himself.

But Meera... Meera wasn't looking at her body.

She was looking under the Car.

"Karan..." Meera called out. "Come here. There's something else."

Karan went there.

Under the Car, where the fuel tank was ruptured, something was written on the ground. In blood.

It wasn't written with their blood. It was written with someone else's blood.

AB KHEL KHATAM (Game Over Now).

And near that writing… a Matchstick lay there.

Not burnt.

Extinguished.

Karan's head spun.

"This matchstick…" Karan picked it up. "It's the same one Vikram threw in the vision."

Meera looked into Karan's eyes. "Karan, if we're dead… then we should have been in 'nark' (hell) or 'swarg' (heaven). Why are we here?"

"Shalini has stopped us," Karan said.

"No," Meera shook her head. "Shalini couldn't stop us. She's just a spirit. Something else… has bound us here."

Just then, from inside that wreckage… Karan's Corpse opened its eyes.

Its eyes were white.

The corpse moved. The sound of crushing metal echoed.

Crrruuunch.

Karan (the spirit) fell back.

The corpse opened its broken mouth and said:

"Because you're not dead yet…

Karan's corpse's lips moved, but the sound wasn't from its throat; it echoed within Karan's (soul's) mind.

Karan (soul) recoiled in fear. "What do you mean? Look at your condition! Your head is split open, your neck is broken. If this isn't death, then what is it?"

The corpse fixed its white eyes on Karan. "This isn't the 'End'. This is a 'Pause'. Time has stopped here. In the outside world… it's still 2:17 AM."

Meera stepped forward, her soul glowing. "So why are we here? In this tunnel?"

"Because we've come to make a decision," Meera's corpse replied from inside the car. She was stuck in the car's wreckage, but her soul stood outside. "Death is a door. Sometimes, it takes time for the door to open."

Suddenly, the sound of petrol leaking from under the car intensified.

Gug-gug-gug…

Karan saw the black oil spreading on the road, slowly advancing towards the engine's hot sparks.

"Understand?" Karan's corpse said. "In the real world, the fuel tank has ruptured. The wiring is short-circuiting. In the next 30 seconds… this car will become a fireball."

Priya shrieked. "So we're going to burn? Like Shalini?"

"You have a choice," the corpse said. "Stay here. As a soul. When the body burns, you won't feel any pain. You will die peacefully. But… you will become a part of this tunnel forever. Like Shalini."

"And the other choice?" Rahul asked, fearfully.

"Go back," the corpse said. "Enter your body."

Everyone fell silent.

"But remember," the corpse warned. "Right now you're not feeling pain because you are separate. The moment you go back inside… you will feel everything. The broken head. The torn skin. The crushed bones. That pain will be so intense that you'll wish you were dead."

Karan looked at his friends.

This was the choice:

Peaceful Death vs Agonizing Survival.

"If we go back," Karan asked, "what guarantee is there that we'll survive? The fire is about to start."

"There's no guarantee," the corpse said. "You'll have to crawl out of the car with that broken body, before the fire starts. Maybe you'll burn. Maybe you'll pass out from the pain. It's a 'Chance'."

Rahul recoiled. "I can't do it. I can't bear the pain. My leg... look how twisted my leg is! I can't go back!"

Priya was crying too. "I'm fine here. It's peaceful here. There's no pain."

Karan looked at them with anger. "So you'll give up? Is this what Shalini wanted! For us to become what she became—a forgotten story?"

Karan turned to Meera. "Meera?"

Meera was staring at the petrol on the road, creeping closer to the sparks.

"We have to fulfill our promise, Karan," Meera said. "We told Shalini we would tell her story to the world. If we die... that promise will be broken. Then we too will be liars."

Meera held Karan's hand. "Pain is only for a few moments. Regret lasts forever."

Karan took a deep breath (which he didn't need to).

"Rahul, Priya," Karan said. "I won't force you. But I'm going back. I'll burn in that fire, but I'll fight. Because I don't want to die a Coward."

Karan moved towards the car.

Meera was with him.

Rahul and Priya looked at each other. The fear within them and the will to live were fighting.

"To hell with the pain," Rahul finally said. "If Karan is going, then so am I. We came together, we'll go together."

Priya also wiped her tears. "I don't want to stay here alone, like a ghost."

The four of them stood near the wreckage.

Their corpses waited for them in front.

"Ready?" Karan asked.

"On three," Rahul said. "One… Two…"

Karan saw that the petrol was about to touch the spark.

"THREE!"

The four of them jumped. Directly into their bodies.

ZAAAP!

Darkness.

And then… A SCREAM.

That sound wasn't a ghost's. It was Karan's own voice.

The moment he entered the body, a sea of pain crashed down on him.

A head-splitting pain.

A sharp stab in the neck.

Lack of air.

The taste of blood in his mouth.

The world was spinning. Everything was blurry.

DUB-DUB… DUB-DUB… (His heartbeat returned).

Karan opened his eyes. This time, real eyes.

One eye was stuck shut with blood. Through the other eye, he saw—that Steering Wheel was pressed into his chest. Breathing was difficult.

"Aaahh…" Karan groaned. Even making a sound was difficult.

Outside… it was dark. Real darkness. No ghostly lights.

Just petrol scattered on the road.

And from under the engine… A spark flew out.

Chitt…

The petrol caught fire.

WHOOSH!

A streak of blue and yellow flames raced beneath the car.

Reality has begun.

Karan was alive. But perhaps only for the next 1 minute.

11

The Escape

PAIN.

Pain.

Only pain.

This was the first signal that hit Karan's mind. His entire body was screaming. His head felt like someone had hit it with a hammer. The pressure of the steering wheel on his chest was so intense that with every breath he took, he could hear his ribs breaking.

"Aaahhh…" A bubble of blood escaped Karan's mouth.

A WHOOSH sound came from outside.

Heat.

Karan opened his blood-clumped eyes. The car was lying upside down. He was hanging from the roof, thanks to his seatbelt.

And outside the windshield… there was fire.

The fire from the petrol tank had now reached the engine. Orange and blue flames were seeping in from beneath the dashboard.

"Need to get out…" Karan's head screamed. "Now"

His trembling hand fumbled for the seatbelt buckle. His fingers weren't working. The buckle was slipping because of the blood.

Click.

The buckle opened.

THUD!

Karan fell straight down (onto what was now the car's roof).

"Aaaarrgh!" his shoulder started paining, maybe it got dislocated.

But there was no time to stop. The fire was now melting the plastic of the dashboard. Toxic smoke was filling the cabin.

"Rahul! Meera!" Karan called caughingly .

A crying sound came from behind him.

"My leg! My leg is stuck!" It was Rahul. His pain was real. His fear was real.

Karan turned, crawling towards the back.

Meera was in the front passenger seat. She was conscious, but in severe shock. Blood was flowing from her forehead.

"Meera, fasten the belt!" Karan shouted.

Meera looked at Karan with numb eyes. "Karan… aag…"

"Yes, fire! Open the buckle!" Karan reached over her and opened her buckle. Meera also fell down with a thump.

"Priya?" Karan looked back.

Priya was unconscious. She was hanging upside down. Rahul was beside her, screaming, clutching his broken leg. The leg that was limping in the 'vision' was, in reality, terribly crushed between the dashboard and the seat.

"Rahul, cut the priya's belt!" Karan ordered.

"I can't move, bhai! It's hurting so much!" Rahul was crying.

The smoke in the cabin had increased so much that visibility was gone. The smell of burning plastic was singeing the hairs in his nose.

Karan picked up a large piece of broken glass from the floor.

“M coming”Karan crawled towards the back. A flame touched the sleeve of his shirt. Karan jerked his hand away and extinguished the fire on his shirt.

He cut Priya’s seatbelt with the piece of glass.

Rrrrip.

Priya fell down, on top of Rahul.

“Sorry Rahul,” Karan said and grabbed Priya by her collar, beginning to drag her towards the window. “Meera, hold her! Pull her out!”

Meera gathered her courage. She grabbed Priya’s hand and started pushing her out through the broken window.

Karan was now with Rahul.

“It will pain,” Karan saw rahul’s leg. Seat’s metal frame had swallowed his leg deeply. “Ready?

“No! Don’t do it!” Rahul screamed.

Karan, ignoring him, tried to pull the seat frame upwards with all his might. Adrenaline surged through his veins.

CREAAAK.

The metal shifted slightly.

“Pull your leg! Now!” Karan yelled.

Rahul screamed as he pulled his leg.

CRACK!

The sound of bone shifting echoed. Rahul was about to pass out from the pain, but Karan slapped him. “Don’t sleep! We need to get out!”

The fire had now caught onto the seats. Karan could feel the heat on his back.

“Come on!”

Karan dragged Rahul to the window. Meera had already escaped with Priya.

Karan pushed Rahul out. Rahul fell onto the road.

Now, only Karan was left inside.

The fire was everywhere. Oxygen was depleting.

Karan started to climb out the window. Half his body was outside.

Just then… he saw something.

On the dashboard inside… lay that photo. Of Shalini and Vikram. Flames were reaching the photo.

For a second, Karan felt as if Shalini was smiling in the photo.

"Go…" a voice whispered.

Karan mustered his last ounce of strength and threw himself out.

He fell onto the road. Scrambling across the concrete, he crawled away from the car.

"Meera! Pull Rahul!"

The four of them—broken, drenched in blood—crawled away from the burning car on the road.

10 meters… 20 meters…

"That's enough!" Karan said and lay down on the ground.

At that very moment… the fire reached the fuel tank.

Karan twisted his neck and looked behind him.

That streak of blue fire underneath the car had now penetrated inside the fuel tank. For a moment, it felt as if time had stopped. The fire went inside and sucked out all the air.

Sssssp…

And then…

BOOM!

The explosion was so powerful it tore the air in the tunnel.

A giant fireball rose into the air. The SUV was ripped to shreds. Iron doors, tyres, glass—everything was flung around like a missile.

The shockwave lifted Karan, Meera, and Rahul off the ground and slammed them several feet forward.

Karan covered his head with his hands. Hot iron and glass rained down from above.

Clang!

Ting!

Thud!

A burning tyre rolled past them.

There was no oxygen in the air now, only fire. The heat was so intense it singed the hair on their eyebrows.

Karan stayed plastered to the ground until the echo of the explosion died down.

Slowly… the noise subsided. Now, only the crackle and roar of the flames could be heard.

Karan lifted his head, coughing.

The scene looked like a war zone.

Where their expensive, luxury SUV had stood, now only a burning iron skeleton remained. The fire was still raging, blackening the tunnel's ceiling.

"Meera? Rahul?" Karan's voice was hoarse. The smoke had scraped his throat raw.

"I'm alive…" Rahul's voice came. He was lying on the ground, holding his broken leg and crying. "Bro, my leg… it hurts so much."

Meera was hunched over Priya, shielding her from the shrapnel. Meera stood up, her face blackened, but she seemed okay.

"We survived," Meera said, looking at the burning car. The reflection danced in her eyes. "We really survived."

Karan tried to stagger to his feet. His whole body ached—broken ribs, a dislocated shoulder, cuts, and bruises.

But this pain… this pain was sweet.

Because this pain was proof of being 'alive'. The numbing cold of the tunnel was gone. Now there was the warmth of fire and the warmth of blood.

"Priya?" Karan asked.

Priya started coughing.

Khukh-Khukh.

She was coming to conscious.

"Water…" Priya whispered.

Karan looked around. There was no water there.

But there was something else.

From the direction of the tunnel's 'Entrance'… light was coming.

This wasn't some ghostly light. This wasn't a flickering sodium light.

This was Red and Blue rotating light.

Wee-woo-Wee-woo-Wee-woo…

The sound of a siren.

Karan's heart pounded hard. Is this another illusion? Is this another ghostly police car?

But just then, the sound of a heavy engine came. A Highway Patrol jeep and an Ambulance sped into the tunnel. The screech of their tyres echoed on the road.

The jeep stopped, and uniformed police personnel got out.

"There are people there!" a constable yelled. "Quick! Bring a stretcher!"

Karan watched the police run towards him. They were real. Their boots made sounds on the road.

His flashlight's beam was flickering.

An inspector reached Karan and held him to prevent him from falling.

"Are you alright, son?" the Inspector asked. "What happened here?"

Karan touched the inspector's uniform. The fabric was rough. Real. He gripped the inspector's hand. It was warm.

Karan started laughing. He laughed like a madman, tears streaming down his face.

"We're alive…" Karan hugged the inspector. "We're alive, Sir! We're alive!"

The inspector looked at him in surprise, then signaled the medical team. "The boy's in shock. Give him oxygen."

Paramedics loaded Rahul onto a stretcher. Rahul was screaming in pain, but the joy of being alive was visible on his face too. Priya and Meera were also wrapped in blankets.

As Karan was being led towards the ambulance, he stopped for a moment.

He turned back and looked at the burning wreckage of the car.

The fire was still raging.

And amidst the smoke of the fire… he saw something.

On the other side of the road, in the darkness, Shalini stood.

She was no longer in her bridal attire. She was in simple white clothes. She wasn't burnt. She was perfectly calm.

Shalini looked at Karan. Then she gave a slight bow—not to thank him, but to bid farewell.

And then, she stepped back into the darkness and vanished.

Karan closed his eyes. “Goodbye, Shalini.”

“Come on, son,” the paramedic said and closed the ambulance door.

The tunnel was left behind.

12

The Reality

Three Days Later.

Karan opened his eyes.

Everything was white. White walls, white ceiling, white sheets.

The air didn't carry that putrid smell of champak and burnt flesh. Instead, there was the sharp, clean scent of Phenyl and Dettol. From somewhere far away, the sound of a machine beeping… beeping… echoed.

Karan tried to move, but a dull pain shot through his ribs. He looked down. Half his body was wrapped in bandages. His hand was in a cast.

"You're awake?"

A soft voice spoke.

Karan turned his head. Meera was standing at the door.

She was in a wheelchair. Her leg was in a cast and there were some cuts on her face, but she was alive. The 'haunting' emptiness was gone from her eyes. There was peace there now.

"Meera…" Karan's voice was hoarse. "Where… where are we?"

"Lilavati Hospital, Mumbai," Meera said, wheeling her chair closer to the bed. "We're home, Karan. Home."

Karan closed his eyes and took a long breath.

Mumbai.

Home.

These words had never tasted so sweet before.

“Rahul? Priya?” Karan asked.

“Priya is fine,” Meera informed him. “She has minor burns and a fracture. She’s in another ward. Rahul…” Meera hesitated a little. “Rahul’s leg… the doctors had to insert a rod. The bone was badly broken. But he’ll be able to walk. It’ll take some time, but he probably won’t be able to run.”

Karan breathed a sigh of relief. “We survived.”

“Yes,” Meera took Karan’s good hand. “You saved us.”

A little while later, a nurse came and gave Karan painkillers. The pain subsided due to the medicine, but his mind was still stuck in the Bhatan Tunnel.

In the evening, Rahul was shifted on a stretcher to Karan’s room so they could all be together. Priya also came, her hand bandaged and a burn mark on her neck—exactly like the one when the ghost had grabbed her.

Rahul looked quite weak, but he gave a faint smile when he saw Karan.

“Bro,” Rahul said slowly. “What happened to my SUV? Will I get insurance?”

Karan and Priya burst out laughing. There was pain in their laughter, but it was the first time they had laughed so freely.

“Forget the car, Rahul,” Karan said. “We’re alive, that’s enough.”

Just then, there was a knock at the door.

An police Inspector entered. The nameplate on his uniform read: Inspector Rane.

Silence fell in the room. The Inspector held a file in his hand.

"Good evening," Inspector Rane said. He looked stern, but there was sympathy in his eyes. "The doctor said you are now in a condition to talk."

"Yes Sir," Karan said, trying to sit up straight on the bed.

The Inspector pulled up a chair and sat down. "First of all, you people are very lucky. The fire that broke out in the Bhatan Tunnel that night… it was impossible to survive in that temperature."

"How did the fire start, Inspector?" Priya asked, though she already knew the answer.

"According to Primary investigation," the Inspector opened the file, "your car's tyre burst. The car skidded and overturned. Fuel leaked, and a short circuit caused a fire. It was a Mechanical Failure."

Karan, Rahul, Meera, and Priya looked at each other.

Mechanical Failure.

How easy those words were.

There were no ghosts in those words. There was no sin in them. There was no regret in them.

"But Sir," the Inspector leaned forward slightly, lowering his voice. "One thing i noticed."

Everyone's ears perked up.

"Your accident happened at 2:17 AM—the car's clock was stopped there," the Inspector said. "And we got a call at 6:00 am from the patrolling jeep who saw the smoke coming."

"So?" Karan asked.

"Sooo…," the Inspector closed the file. "From 2 am to 6 am…Four hours, The car's engine was hot, petrol was leaking. Technically, the car should have caught fire within 5 minutes of the accident. According to the physics, it's impossible for the fire to 'wait' for 4 hours and then ignite when you all regained consciousness."

The Inspector looked at them intently. "It looks like… something held the fire back. Like someone wants you guys to come out safely."

Meera squeezed Karan's hand.

"Maybe we were lucky," Karan lied. He couldn't tell the police about 'Shalini'. They would think he was crazy.

The Inspector stood up. "Well, whatever it is. The case has been closed. 'Accidental Fire'. You guys have rest."

The Inspector walked to the door, then stopped.

"By the way," the Inspector turned around. "The spot where your accident happened… there was an accident there 7 years ago as well.. Same spot. A girl died there. Her name was Shalini."

Priya's face turned white.

"We know," Priya said softly.

The Inspector nodded. "The strange thing is… since that night, accidents in that tunnel have increased. People used to say there was something 'negative' there. But after your accident…"

The Inspector smiled and said.

"In the past three days, there haven't been any accidents. The patrol team says the tunnel now… Seems quiet. As if some 'burden' has been lightened."

Tears welled up in Karan's eyes.

"Thanks, Inspector," Karan said.

After the Inspector left, there was a deep peace in the room.

Shalini was gone. forever.

But their work was not finished yet.

Priya picked up her phone from her side table (which was new, the old one had been left in the tunnel).

"Karan," Priya said. There was a new strength in her voice. "I want to write a story."

"Which story?" Rahul asked.

"True Story," Priya said. "The story of MLA Deshmukh's son. Shalini's story. I will write that article again. This time without taking money. This time without fear."

"But your career?" Meera asked worriedly. "They will try to kill you."

"Let them do it," Priya said with a smile. "One who has come back after touching death is not afraid of threats. We made a promise to Shalini: 'Truth sets us free.'"

Karan looked at Priya and felt proud.

"We are all together in this," Karan said. "We will all be witnesses. This time, Shalini will get justice."

They held each other's hands.

These four friends, who had just set out on a weekend trip, had now changed.

There were marks on their bodies that would probably heal.

But the marks on their souls would forever remind them that between Life and Death, there's only one 'Truth' that stands between them.

Epilogue

Six Months Later

MUMBAI MIRROR - FRONT PAGE HEADLINE:

"BHATAN TUNNEL MURDER CASE REOPENED: MLA'S SON VIKRAM DESHMUKH ARRESTED."

By Priya Sharma, Senior Correspondent.

"Seven years ago, a file was closed, dismissed as an 'accident'. Today, it has risen from the ashes. Following forensic reports and new witness testimonies, police have confirmed that Shalini Mehta's death was no accident, but a premeditated conspiracy..."

Karan folded the newspaper and placed it on the dashboard.

There was a peace on his face, seen for the first time in six months. He wasn't in a suit-boot anymore; he wore a simple cotton shirt. The hustle and bustle of corporate life no longer appealed to him. After staring death in the face, the meaning of 'deadlines' had changed.

"Ready?" Karan asked.

From the back seat, Rahul replied, "Always ready, Bro."

Rahul's voice still held that old enthusiasm, but he now walked with a limp. There was a steel rod in his leg. That rod was a constant reminder that speed isn't always thrilling.

Priya was sitting in the passenger seat. She had her new camera hanging around her neck. She had written that article. The

MLA's goons had threatened her, broken her home windows, but this time Priya didn't stop. She did what she should have done seven years ago.

And Meera… Meera was looking out the window, smiling.

"Let's go," Meera said. "She must be waiting."

Karan started the car. This wasn't an SUV. It was a simple sedan.

They took the Mumbai-Pune Expressway. The same road. The same wind.

But today there was no fear.

When the entrance of Bhatan Tunnel appeared, silence fell over the car. Everyone's heartbeats quickened slightly, due to old memories.

The car entered the tunnel.

Whoosh.

The sunlight outside vanished, and those familiar yellow sodium lights came on.

But today the lights weren't flickering.

There was no static on the radio.

There was no foul, rotting smell in the air.

The tunnel was just… a tunnel. Concrete and asphalt. Lifeless.

Karan slowed the car and stopped at the exact spot where their accident had happened. Where their car had burned.

The road had been repaired now. The burn marks had been removed. New paint had been applied.

All four of them got out of the car.

Traffic was moving through the tunnel. Cars zoomed past them. No one stopped, but this time, it no longer caused sorrow. Life must go on.

Meera took a bouquet of flowers from her bag.

White Roses.

She went to the side of the road, where an old, blackened 'Milestone' stood.

Meera placed the flowers there.

"You are free, Shalini," Meera whispered. "Vikram is in jail. The world knows the truth. Your story is no longer 'incomplete'."

Priya wiped her eyes. "Sorry, Shalini. For being late."

Rahul, putting weight on his injured leg, said, "And thanks. For giving us another chance. We won't waste it."

Karan stood there, looking up at the tunnel's ceiling.

He remembered that fire, those screams, that pain. But then he remembered that final moment—when Shalini had bowed her head and bid them farewell.

"Shall we go?" Karan asked.

"Let's go," Meera said.

They got back in the car.

As soon as Karan started the engine, a gust of cool wind came in through the open window.

There was a chill in this wind, but it wasn't biting. This wind was like someone's blessing.

And in that wind… there was the scent of Jasmine. A soft, sweet fragrance.

Meera smiled. "She's happy."

Karan put the car in gear and drove forward.

The tunnel's exit was visible ahead. White light.

This time, that light was real.

The car exited the tunnel and was lost in the sunlight.

Behind it, Bhatan Tunnel stood in its place—calm, silent, and now… Sacred.

The road kept going. The journey continued.

Because there is no such thing as an end. There is only a new beginning.

Author's Note

This story was written as a work of fiction.

It does not attempt to document, investigate, or explain any real incidents, beliefs, or folklore associated with Bhatan Tunnel or its surroundings.

The fear explored here is not about places.
It is about choices. About what we ignore.
About what we leave behind.

Some journeys end not because the road disappears, but because we refuse to stop.

If this story stayed with you,

a review helps it find the right readers.

About GullyShelf

GullyShelf Collective is an independent publishing imprint focused on stories rooted in lived experience, emotional truth, and cultural memory.

The Collective curates fiction and narrative work that values atmosphere over spectacle, restraint over excess, and intention over volume. Each title is selected not for trends, but for its ability to stay with the reader long after the final page.

GullyShelf Collective publishes a limited list, working closely with authors whose voices align with its editorial vision—stories that travel quietly, but leave a lasting imprint.

More titles from **GullyShelf Collective** coming soon.

About the Author

Abhay Singhaal is an Indian storyteller whose work explores psycho- logical fear, human denial, and the thin line between logic and belief.

His stories are grounded in real landscapes, everyday people, and the quiet dread that hides beneath ordinary journeys.

The Last Ride Through Bhatan Tunnel is his horror debut.

9 788199 823532

Printed at Repro India Ltd.